Fiction for Girls

by

Jane Sorenson

It's Me, Jennifer
It's Your Move, Jennifer
Jennifer's New Life
Jennifer Says Goodbye
Boy Friend
Once Upon a Friendship
Fifteen Hands
In Another Land
The New Pete
Out with the In Crowd
Another Jennifer
Family Crisis

Hi, I'm Katie Hooper
Home Sweet Haunted Home
Happy Birth Day
Honor Roll
First Job
Angels on Holiday
The New Me
Left Behind

Left Behind

by Jane Sorenson

illustrated by Kathleen L. Smith

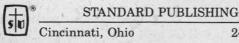
STANDARD PUBLISHING
Cincinnati, Ohio   24-03964

LIBRARY OF CONGRESS
Library of Congress Cataloging-in-Publication Data

Sorensen, Jane.
    Left behind / by Jane Sorenson ; illustrated by Kathleen L. Smith.
        p.   cm. — (A Katie Hooper book ; 8)
    Summary: When her best friend moves away in the summer, Katie
worries about making new friends.
    ISBN 0-87403-564-3
    [1. Moving, Household—Fiction. 2. Friendship—Fiction.
3. Christian life—Fiction.] I. Smith, Kathleen L., 1950- ill.
II. Title. III. Series: Sorenson, Jane. Katie Hooper book ; 8.
PZ7.S7214Le 1989
[Fic]—dc19   89-4527
                                                                  CIP
                                                                   AC

With love
to Mel Sorenson,

my dear husband and best friend,
who generously supplies me with
both love and encouragement

Summer Vacation Begins

Nothing was happening at my house when Sara Wilcox and I finished walking my dog January. Purple Jeep was gone, which probably meant Dad had taken off to paint a mountain. Frankly, it doesn't seem possible that we've lived in this old wreck of a house for almost a year. Now my best friend and I sat down on the back steps.

"Just think," I said. "An entire summer with nothing to do! I can't believe school is actually over!"

"Not nothing to do, Katie," Sara corrected, a huge smile on her face. "A summer when we can do anything we want!"

"Right," I said. "Any ideas?"

"Not exactly," she said. "But don't worry! We'll think of something!"

"Some of the kids are taking trips," I said. "Did you hear that Christopher and his father are spending a couple of weeks surfing in California? And Kimberly Harris is going to visit her old friends in Philadelphia."

"Do you think she might move back?"

"I doubt it," I said. "Hey, Sara! I just got an idea! While Kimberly's there, I think I'll ask her to call my cousin Jennifer. I think that's where my cousins live."

"Why not?" Sara said, smiling. "You could get lucky. Maybe your cousin will invite you to visit her! Katie, you might finally get to go somewhere!"

"I didn't think of that."

Sara's eyes got big. "You could even fly on an airplane!"

I shook my head. "No way! We could never afford that. Are you sure it's too far to drive?"

"I'm positive!" Sara said. "Driving would take forever. Frankly, I can't believe you've never set foot in another state!"

"I could do worse," I said. "I happen to like Colorado. I guess you think you're some kind of world traveler—just because you used to live in Omaha!"

"Well, it's a start!" Sara said. "Katie, you'll see!

Someday I am going to travel all over the country!" Her eyes got big. "Maybe even all over the world!"

"Sure," I said, watching as January tried to get away from a butterfly. "In the meantime, do you want to eat lunch at my house? I'm sure Mom won't mind."

"I have a better idea!" she said. "Why don't you come home with me?"

I nearly fainted. The truth is, I've only eaten lunch at Sara's house once.

"I know it's pretty incredible!" Sara grinned. "But Mom's actually there! She doesn't start work today until one o'clock."

"I'll ask my mother," I told her.

Mom reminded me I had to babysit this afternoon. After ditching the dog, Sara and I headed for the small house where she lives with her mother. Although it was no big deal, I felt excited.

"Hi, Katie," Mrs. Wilcox said, smiling. "How's life at the Spook House?"

"Fine," I said. "But we don't call it that anymore! Mostly I call it Home Sweet Home."

"Excuse me!" Sara's mother laughed. "Then how are things at Home Sweet Home?"

"The usual," I said. "Well, actually, it's pretty busy. Dad's illustrating a book. Jason's got a job helping Sam Johnson. And this afternoon I have

9

to babysit Amy while Mom checks out a wall-paper job."

Mrs. Wilcox smiled. "How is the baby? I haven't seen your sister in months!"

"She's standing up already," I said proudly. "Mom thinks she'll be an early walker."

"I invited Katie for lunch," Sara said. "It's OK, isn't it?"

Mrs. Wilcox hesitated. "Why, of course, Sara. But you know it's nothing special—just peanut butter and jelly."

I laughed. "That's mostly what we have too!"

In a few minutes, we all sat down at the kitchen table. I noticed that all the silverware matched, and every knife pointed straight forward. We even had placemats that matched the plates! But we didn't pray. After watching Sara take a bite, I began to eat too.

"It seems funny for me to have lunch at home," Mrs. Wilcox said. "I've gotten used to eating my noon meal at the restaurant."

"How come your schedule changed?" I asked.

"Business is slow," Sara's mother said. "I guess people don't have money to eat out."

"Mom's worried," Sara announced.

"Everybody is," her mother said. "Another plant in Colorado Springs closed last week. There must be hundreds of people looking for jobs!"

Although I felt sorry for them, I couldn't think of anything to say. The truth is, my father has never had a regular job. So I decided to change the subject. I smiled. "Did Sara tell you my teacher's getting married?"

"How nice!" Mrs. Wilcox smiled.

"Actually, *my* teacher introduced them!" Sara bragged.

"Her name won't be Ms. Allen anymore," I said. "Starting next week she'll be Mrs. Mc-Mann!"

"Will it be a big wedding?" Mrs. Wilcox asked.

"I think so! She invited every kid in our room!"

"You didn't tell me that!" Sara said. "Katie, I didn't know you were going!"

"I didn't want you to feel left out," I explained. "Actually, I got a regular invitation in the mail and everything!"

"I've never been to a wedding," Sara said. "You'll have to tell me all about it."

"I planned to."

"Will it be at your church?" Mrs. Wilcox asked.

I shook my head. "It's going to be outdoors, in Mr. Campbell's yard. Ms. Allen says she's always wanted a garden wedding."

Sara's face clouded up. "What if it rains?"

"In Colorado it doesn't rain a lot," I explained.

"But what if it does?" Sara asked again.

11

"I'm glad it isn't my problem!" said Sara's mother.

"You don't have to worry," Sara said. "Personally, I'm having a big church wedding!"

"I thought you quit worrying about romance and boyfriends," I said.

"I'm not worrying about them." Sara grinned. "But it never hurts to have goals! After I finish college, I'll work a few years. And then I'm getting married. In a church!"

"You can't always control your life like that," her mother told her.

"I thought you've always wanted me to go to college," Sara said. "So I won't have to wait tables."

"I do want you to have a good career," Mrs. Wilcox said. "I believe all girls should have goals. But nobody can control the future! My whole life changed when your father died!"

"Dad says God controls the future," I said. "He says the Lord has a plan for everyone's life."

"Right," said Mrs. Wilcox. But I don't think she really believed it.

"Did God really know all those people were going to be out of work?" Sara asked.

"He had to know it," I said. "He knows everything."

Sara stopped eating. "Then why didn't He stop the plants from closing?"

12

"I'm not sure," I said.

"Come to think of it," Sara said, "if God knows everything, how come He let my father die?"

Mrs. Wilcox was listening. I felt my face getting red. Here was my big chance to say something wonderful about the Lord in front of Sara's mother. And I didn't have a clue as to what it should be!

"I don't know," I said.

"Then maybe I'll ask Mayblossom McDuff at Sunday school. Or maybe I'll even ask the Lord Himself!"

"Sara, don't be rude!" Her mother looked horrified.

Sara pressed her lips together and didn't say another word.

Mrs. Wilcox forced a smile. "You girls have a nice afternoon. I have to go to work now."

"Thanks for having me over, Mrs. Wilcox!" I said. "Your peanut butter was delicious!"

Now her smile became more natural. "It's nothing! Please come again! Why, Sara's practically lived over at your house ever since you moved here!"

I laughed. "My brother's always teasing me that Sara and I are together so much we're going to turn into twins! But so far my hair hasn't turned red!"

After she left, the little kitchen seemed very

13

quiet. We loaded the dishwasher, and then Sara hid the placemats in a drawer. You'd never know anyone ate there. What a contrast to the scene at my house!

Suddenly Sara broke into a big smile. "I've got an idea!" she said. "Katie, I just thought of a way I can go to Ms. Allen's wedding!"

We Remember an Old Idea

Once you get to know Sara Wilcox, you realize she's a never-ending fountain of ideas and schemes. Not only that, but Sara can talk people into almost anything! So I wasn't really too surprised to hear she had a plan to attend the wedding.

"I'll take pictures!" Sara said. "Every bride wants pictures of her wedding!"

"Are you good enough?" I asked. "Be honest, Sara. You've never taken pictures, have you?"

"The camera's automatic!" She grinned. "How hard can it be?"

I thought a minute, remembering when we first won our cameras by selling candy. "Sara, maybe we can do it together!" I said. "We talked

15

about becoming photographers. What happened?"

"We got too busy!" she said. "But aren't you glad we waited? This will be the perfect thing to do this summer! And I can use the money. Obviously, I can't clear the snow from people's driveways anymore!"

"Sara, do you really think people will pay us to take pictures?"

"I don't see why not!" she said. "And once we get our start at the wedding, we'll have some professional experience!"

"Does your mother have wedding pictures?" I asked.

Sara smiled. "Frankly, that's what gave me the idea!" she said. "Mom just brought out a picture I've never seen before. I think she must have hidden it away when my father died. Come on! I'll show you!"

I followed her into her mother's bedroom with its white furniture and pink bedspread. On the dresser was a large framed photograph. I was impressed with the flowing white dress and the tuxedo. But mostly I studied the faces. "Wow! She looks beautiful! And your father sure is handsome!" I smiled. "Sara, now I know where you got your curly red hair!"

Sara nodded. "Katie, how about you? Have you seen your parents' wedding pictures?"

"Mom and Dad didn't have a fancy wedding. Actually, they eloped!"

Sara's eyes got big. "Wow! How come?"

"Mom's parents didn't want her to marry my father," I explained. "To be honest, they didn't think his dream of painting mountains was very practical. But Mom loved Dad so much she came to Colorado with him anyway!"

"How romantic!" Sara sighed.

"All they have from their wedding is a snapshot taken by their friends," I said. "But Mom has it framed."

"Katie, do your parents still look the same?"

"Kind of," I said. "I think Mom must have been born tall and slender! And I'd recognize Dad's smile anywhere!"

"I'm curious," Sara said. "Back then, did your father have more hair?"

"Lots more!" I laughed. "Why?"

"No offense, Katie," Sara said. "But I could never elope with a guy who was getting bald!"

"Dad wasn't getting bald!" I said. "In those days, most guys wore their hair real long! Anyhow, I don't think they lose their hair when they're that young! Have you ever seen a bald teenager?"

"Good point!" Sara laughed. "Anyhow, now all I have to do is convince Ms. Allen she needs me to take wedding pictures!"

17

"Count me in too!" I said. "Sara, don't forget, we planned to do it together! I know as much about taking pictures as you do!"

Sara looked at me. "So when are you going to ask her?"

"Ask who?"

"Ms. Allen," Sara said. "Can you call her this afternoon?"

"How come I have to do it?" I asked. "Don't forget, you're the born salesperson!"

"Well," Sara said, "after all, she is your teacher!"

"Oh, no! Sara, I'll see you later!" Suddenly, I remembered I was supposed to babysit.

When I got home, Mom was waiting for me. "I won't be long," she said. "I'm just going to measure so Kimberly's mother will know how many rolls of wallpaper to order."

Lots of people are moving to Woodland Park, Colorado. Last year, Sara came here from Omaha. My own family moved into town from a cabin up in the mountains. And Kimberly Harris moved from Philadelphia into a huge brand-new house with three bathrooms.

By the time I met Kimberly, Sara and I were already best friends. To be completely honest, in the beginning I didn't exactly like Kimberly much anyhow. But now, after a rocky start at school, she's fitting in much better.

When Mrs. Harris arrived to pick up Mom, Kimberly was sitting in the front seat. "Hi, Katie!" she yelled.

I followed Mom out to the car. "Hi, Kimberly! How do you like being out of school?"

"It's OK," she said. "Well, to be honest, I'm bored already! I can hardly wait to visit all my old friends in Philadelphia!"

"Kimberly, will you do me a favor?" I smiled. "While you're there, could you call my cousin?"

"Where does she live?"

I looked at my mother. "Mom, where does Jennifer Green live?"

"Somewhere near Valley Forge," Mom said. "I think it's called Berwyn. Why?"

Kimberly squealed. "No kidding! That's real close to where I used to live!"

"You'll do it then?" I asked.

"Sure!" Kimberly smiled. "Just get me the phone number. I'll be glad to call her!" As I watched the car drive off, I got excited. I've never met one of my relatives. Why, there could be lots of them!

Now, however, I turned to another problem. I had no idea where I put my camera. To be honest, I've never used it. Although I was super excited when I won it, I've never even bought any film!

While Amy slept, I quietly poked around my

19

room. Although I keep trying to change, eventually my room always ends up in a state of disaster! Under the bed I found a lot of dust and my valentine from Christopher Bean. My Bic pen turned up in a pile of dirty underwear. But I never did find my camera. At least I didn't find it by the time my sister woke from her nap.

"Hi, Little Sugarplum!" I said.

The baby grinned at me.

"Mom's checking out wallpaper at Kimberly's house," I told her. "So you're in luck! Want to help me find my camera?"

Amy gurgled. After I changed her diaper, I stuck her on a blanket in the middle of my floor. But she wouldn't stay there! Once I found her under my desk trying to eat a green crayon!

"Amy! That's not what it's for!" I laughed. "It's for coloring! Here! I'll show you!"

By the time I decided Amy was too little to color, I had given up on the camera. "Come on, Amy!" I said. "Let's have a snack! And then I'm taking you outside!" Down in the kitchen, I poured her a cup of apple juice.

"Katie! Katie Hooper!" Sara called through the screen door. "Are you home?"

"Come on in!" I yelled.

"I can't! It's hooked!"

At that point, January started to howl. *Aaaaaooooooo! AaaaaaOooooo!* I couldn't believe

20

it! He hadn't gone into his "Star Spangled Banner" routine in months! "Quit it!" I said, grabbing for him. He thought it was a game. *AaaaaaOoooo!*

"Are you coming, or not?" called Sara.

"Da, da, da, da!" said the grinning baby. And then she knocked over her juice.

Finally, Sara and I got everything cleaned up. "My house is so boring!" she said. "I knew I could find some excitement over here! Oh, I almost forgot! I brought my camera!"

"This won't make a good picture!" I told her. "The kitchen's too messy!"

Sara paid no attention. She pointed the camera at January, who was trying to curl up under Amy's highchair. The dog winked at her. "Hold it!" Sara yelled.

We heard a click.

"Oh, no!" Sara said. "The flash didn't go off!"

"Too bad."

"How about bringing Amy outdoors?" Sara asked. "Then I wouldn't need a flash."

"Actually, we were going out anyway," I said. I carried the baby out to the stroller.

Sara sat on the porch steps and pointed her camera at my sister. Amy and I waited and waited while Sara just sat there squinting into the little window. Finally, I couldn't stand it any longer. "Now what's wrong?"

"She isn't smiling," Sara said.

"Hi, Amy!" I waved my arms and made faces. I mean, I tried everything! But do you think that baby would smile now? Of course not!

"I'm in no rush!" Sara said, finally. "I have all afternoon. I'll just wait here until she does it! But in the meantime, Katie, why don't you call Ms. Allen?"

We Stop at the Restaurant

Even if she is my best friend, I hate it when Sara makes me feel like I have no choice! And I also hated the idea of calling Ms. Allen. I stood there in front of the phone trying to decide which was worse—bugging Ms. Allen or having Sara bug me! Finally, I looked up my teacher's number and dialed.

"Hello," said a familiar voice.

"Hi, Ms. Allen. It's Katie Hooper." I took a deep breath. "I was just wondering. How are things coming with your wedding plans?"

"Everything's wonderful, Katie!"

"I'm glad," I said. "Can I ask you something? I don't suppose you need anyone to take pictures?"

"A photographer's coming up from the Springs," Ms. Allen told me. "And Mr. Campbell's going to get it on video. Why, Katie?"

"Well, my friend Sara Wilcox was just wondering if she could take pictures. But it sounds to me like you're all set."

"Well, I guess we could use some informal snapshots," Ms. Allen said. I could hear the smile in her voice.

"Actually, Sara and I were thinking of doing it together," I admitted. "Last fall we both won cameras in the school candy sale."

"I remember," Ms. Allen said.

"Then we can do it? It's really OK?" I couldn't believe it!

"I've been trying to think of ways to involve some of the students in the wedding," Ms. Allen said. "I think you've helped me out!"

"No kidding!"

"Katie, there's just one thing." Now she was using her school-teacher voice. "I've already told Mr. Campbell I don't want anything to disrupt the ceremony. I'd hate to have flashbulbs going off or people running up the aisle."

"Oh, we wouldn't do that!" I promised. "You can count on me!"

"I know I can," my teacher said. "Katie, you've never let me down!"

I wanted to run and tell Sara. But to be honest, I didn't know how to end the conversation. "I guess you won't be Ms. Allen much longer."

"That's right. After next week, I'll be Ms. Mc-Mann!"

"Ms. McMann!" I said. "I thought for sure you'd be Mrs. McMann!"

She laughed. "Thanks for calling, Katie! I'll see you soon."

"You're welcome!" I said, grinning from ear to ear. Then I raced out the door.

"She said we can do it!" I told Sara. "As long as we don't interrupt the ceremony!"

"Super!" Sara seemed relieved. "Who says you aren't a good salesperson! By the way, Katie, your sister finally smiled!"

"When you get a print made, can I have a copy?" I asked.

"There won't be any picture," Sara said.

"Why not?"

Sara's smile faded. "Because I was just practicing, that's why! I don't have any film in the camera! Hey, why don't we go downtown and get some?"

As soon as my mother got home, Sara and I took off for the Ben Franklin. We each bought a roll of film.

"Will twelve pictures be enough?" I asked.

"Of course not," Sara said. "But we need to practice so we'll get the hang of it. If we fumble around getting the camera loaded or something, it will be pretty embarrassing!"

I agreed. "Does the instruction book show how to do everything?"

"Sure!" she said. "All we have to do is look at the pictures."

Frankly, I hated to confess that I had lost my instruction book—along with my camera! It would turn up somewhere. "Do we have to go right home?" I asked.

"What did you have in mind?"

I glanced over at the restaurant. "Maybe we could stop and see your mother."

"Why not!" she said. "Mom says there's never much business in the afternoon." When we first entered the restaurant, I didn't see anybody, not even Mrs. Wilcox. But as the door closed, Sara's mother stood up next to a booth on the right. She smiled when she saw us. "Hi, girls!" Then she turned and spoke to someone in the booth. "It's my daughter."

"Hi, Mom!" Sara said. "We were just downtown buying film for our cameras. Hope you don't mind that we stopped by!"

"Of course not," her mother said. "Come over here. I want to introduce you to someone."

Sitting with his back toward the door was a round-faced man. He looked up from his coffee and smiled.

"I'd like you to meet Ernie Kennedy," said Mrs. Wilcox. "Ernie, this is my daughter, Sara." She turned to me. "And this is her friend, Katie Hooper."

"Hi," said the man.

"It's a small world," Sara told him. "My grandmother in Omaha was named Kennedy."

"So I've heard," he said. "In fact, that's how your mother and I first got acquainted."

Mrs. Wilcox seemed embarrassed. "I just happened to mention that my name used to be Karen Kennedy."

"That was long ago," Sara said. "Back before you got married."

"Can I get you girls something cold to drink?" Mrs. Wilcox asked.

"My treat," the man said.

"You don't have to do that, Ernie." Mrs. Wilcox smiled at him.

"No problem! I can afford a couple of soft drinks." He smiled. "Would you girls like to join us?"

I didn't know what to say. I looked at Sara. "No thanks," she told him. "We'll sit at the counter."

Even when Mrs. Wilcox smiled and put large Cokes in front of us, I could tell that Sara was not happy. "How come you have to tell our life history to a perfect stranger?" she asked.

Her mother leaned down and talked softly. "Ernie isn't a stranger, Sara," she said. "For weeks now, he's been coming in every afternoon for coffee."

"Why isn't he at work?" Sara asked.

I sipped my Coke and listened. Frankly, I had no choice.

"Shhh!" Mrs. Wilcox said. "He lost his job. And he's having a hard time finding another one. I've been trying to encourage him!" She smoothed her apron with her hands and headed over to Ernie's booth.

"It's no big deal," I said. "Your mother's just being friendly!"

"That's easy for you to say," Sara said. "What if it were your mother?"

Sara was right. It's hard for me to imagine my mother as a waitress. But actually, Mom happens to be very encouraging herself! I don't know what Dad would do if she weren't!

I decided to change the subject. "Sara, guess what Ms. Allen's new husband looks like!" I had already met him!

"Tall and handsome!" Sara said, grinning. "Grooms are supposed to be tall and handsome!"

"They can't all start out like that," I said. "After all, how many fathers are tall and handsome? Being married can't change them that much!"

Sara giggled. "Good point!"

I was glad she agreed with me. "I think it's more important whether they're nice or not!" I said, going strong. "After all, the Lord judges people on how they look inside!"

"That's all right for Him!" Sara said. "But personally, I hope He gives me somebody tall and handsome!"

Because I wasn't watching, I slurped up the last of my drink and made a noise.

"Katie, let's go home," Sara said. "I'm anxious to try loading the cameras!"

When Ernie Kennedy saw us getting ready to leave, he stood up. And that's when we realized how short he is! "Good-bye, Sara and Katie!" He smiled. "It was nice to meet you!"

"Thanks for the Cokes!" I told him.

Sara didn't say anything. But once we got across the street, she could hardly stand it. "What a shrimp!" she giggled. "Ernie Kennedy reminds me of a cuddly teddy bear!"

"So what's the difference?" I said. "He bought us Cokes, didn't he?"

We Try Praying

"So, I thought we were going to take pictures together," Sara said, when we finished putting film in her camera.

"We are," I told her. "But I can learn a lot just from watching you!"

"I know what you're doing!" Sara said. "You're just saving your film! Then when mine's all gone, you'll still be able to take pictures!"

I took a deep breath. "I might as well tell you," I said. "I can't find my camera!"

She just looked at me. "What do you mean? Katie, you've never even used it!"

"It isn't really lost," I told her. "It has to be some place!"

"I can't understand it, Katie," she said. "Why

31

don't you just put your things away?"

"Sara, get off my case!" I told her. "Don't you think I know that!"

Silently we sat together on the back steps. Finally Sara had an idea. "Katie, why don't you pray?" she said. "I'll never forget how you found January right after you prayed!"

"I might as well," I said. "I've looked everywhere."

Frankly, I'm amazed at how much Sara Wilcox knows about the Lord! Why, when she first moved here, I even had to tell her that Jesus is a real person! But from the beginning, Sara's had no trouble believing in prayer!

"I'll handle it," Sara said, closing her eyes. "Lord Jesus, please help Katie find her camera! Amen." She opened her eyes. "Whoops!" She closed her eyes again. "I forgot to tell You, she needs it before the wedding!"

I opened my eyes and grinned.

"Don't worry!" Sara said. "You'll find it!"

"Sara, you don't have to wait for me! Why don't you go ahead and take pictures?"

"It won't be as much fun!" she said. "Best friends do things together! Right?"

I laughed. "OK, Sara. Let's jog!"

"You would pick that!" She laughed too. It's about the only activity we don't share! "I know! Let's work on our quilts!"

"Super!" I said. "After lunch!"

Later, I looked up and watched Sara stick a blue calico star in the center of a white square. OK, so her stitches are kind of big and crooked! I bet you'd never guess Mom even had to teach her how to hold a needle!

Not to brag, but my own quilt is bigger, with hearts on it—because my Hooper family symbol is a heart. When Sara found out, she wanted a symbol too. She picked a star because she wants to be an actress.

"I hope sewing the squares together will be easier," Sara said. "I hate these points!"

"You should try these curves!" I said. "If I'm not careful, people will think my symbol is a banana!"

She laughed. "Speaking of symbols, your teacher's going to love the potholders you made for her wedding present!"

"It was Mom's idea," I said. "She thought if I shaped them like hearts, Ms. Allen would remember I made them."

"You're lucky, Katie!" Sara said. "I wish my birthday were on Valentine's day!"

"Mom says every birthday is special!" I told her. "By the way, Sara, when's yours?"

"August eighth," she said. "It was just before you moved here."

"Oh," I said. As I remembered how everyone

surprised me back in February, suddenly I had an idea! Why, I could give a surprise party for Sara! I felt so excited that it was hard to keep from smiling and giving it all away!

Later, while I was helping Mom with dinner, I asked her about my cousin. "Do you think Jennifer might invite me to come for a visit?"

"Don't count on it," Mom said. "Besides, even if she did, we don't have the money to travel that far!"

"When I see big families at church, sometimes I feel jealous," I admitted. "Michelle's cousins get together almost every Sunday!"

"You have Sara," Mom said. "And the Lord has given us a church family. Would you like to have Mayblossom McDuff and everybody come for a picnic on the Fourth of July?"

"All right!" I said, remembering when we included all our friends last Christmas. "But Mom, is it wrong to want real relatives?"

Mom put her hand on my shoulder. "Of course not, Katie!" she said. "I wish it were different too! But even if your father weren't so stubborn, we still live thousands of miles apart!"

"How old is Jennifer?" I asked.

"She's older than you are," Mom said. "I think her brothers would be closer to your age."

"What are my cousins like?"

Mom smiled. "You'd like them! Of course, I've

only met them once, when I went to Illinois for your grandfather's funeral. But Jennifer is just as open and honest as you are, Katie! Pete's tall and serious. And I think Justin's into sports."

"Are they Christians?"

"I think so, but I don't know. The Greens live in a different world, Katie! They have lots of money!"

I watched Mom's face. "And how about my grandmother?"

Mom's eyes filled with tears, just as I knew they would. "I miss her very much," she said. "When I went back for Grandpa Green's funeral, we worked things out. But, Katie, your father is a proud man!"

"Maybe we should pray about it," I said.

"I've been praying for many years!" Mom sighed. "Katie, I haven't let this ruin my life! I have so much to be thankful for!"

"But you'll still give me Jennifer's phone number, won't you?"

"Of course." Mom smiled. "There's just one problem. I seem to have lost my address book!"

"I can't believe it! I lost my camera! Mom, do you think losing things is a disease?"

"Who knows?" Mom said. "When I started out, I was so determined to put my family ahead of perfect housekeeping. But I'm afraid I went too far the other way!"

"I really need the camera!" I said. "Sara and I are taking pictures at Ms. Allen's wedding!"

"Oh, my," Mom said. "Maybe we should pray about it."

"I already did," I said. "Have you prayed about the address book?"

Mom grinned. "No, but I'll do it right now!"

I guess someone who doesn't believe in the power of prayer would say that we would have found the things anyway. But I know God had a hand in it! It turned out that Dad had borrowed Mom's address book. And my camera was in a drawer in the keeping room. "I didn't hide it," my brother said. "I just didn't want it to get wrecked when Sam Johnson was installing the wood stove!"

After we finished the dishes, I couldn't wait to call Sara. "Guess what! I found it! My brother stuck it in a drawer in the keeping room!"

"That's good," Sara said. Her voice sounded soft and flat.

"Sara, what's wrong?"

"Nothing."

"Come on!" I urged. "You can tell me! I'm your best friend! Remember?"

"Can I come over?" she asked.

"Sure," I said. "I'll meet you on the porch steps."

I watched her make her way up the path.

Frankly, I've never seen her look like this.

"Is your mother sick?" I asked.

"Just be still and let me tell it!" she said.

So I sat there and waited.

"As soon as my mother came home, I knew something was up!" Sara told me. "First Mom said how glad she was that we had stopped in to see her at the restaurant. Then she went on and on about how much that guy Ernie Kennedy liked me."

I nodded my head and waited.

"This is hard," Sara said, swallowing.

"Is your mother sick?" I asked again.

She shook her head. "It's worse that that! That little guy actually invited Mom to go to a movie! In Colorado Springs!"

"No kidding!" I said. "Ernie Kennedy asked your mother for a date?"

Sara nodded. "Wait until you hear the worst part!"

"Yes?"

"Mom's going!"

Here Comes the Bride!

During the next week, Sara and I each took a practice roll of pictures. We also worked on our quilts, and we laid out our outfits for the wedding. But mostly Sara fumed about Ernie Kennedy.

"Mom's never home!" Sara said. "I mean it was bad enough when she worked all the time. But now she spends her free time with him!"

"Come on, Sara," I said. "They've only gone out three times!"

"It seems like more," she said.

"Is your mother happy?"

Sara thought about it. "I have to admit she's never seemed happier. But how about me? Don't I count?"

"Sara, you're happy when you aren't thinking about it, aren't you?"

"I guess so. But that's the trouble!" she said. "I think about it all the time!"

"Let's try thinking about the wedding," I said. "Are you sure my shoes are all right?"

"Well, white might be better!" she told me. "But frankly, Katie, no one's going to be looking at your feet!"

I grinned. "You're probably right! Besides, I don't have any white shoes anyway!"

Well, as it turned out, Sara was absolutely right about the possibility of the weather causing problems. On the day of the wedding, I was awakened by rain pounding against my window. "Oh, no, Lord!" I said. "Please don't let rain spoil the wedding!"

"Do they have alternate plans?" Mom asked, as we ate our weekly pancake breakfast.

"I have no idea," I told her. "I just know that Ms. Allen always wanted a garden wedding."

"Sometimes our plans get spoiled," Dad said. "Sometimes it rains."

"Maybe they rented a tent," my brother said. "That's what I would have done!"

The telephone rang. It was Sara. "Now what are we going to do?" she asked. "I don't want my camera to get all wet!"

All day, the only thing on my mind was poor

Ms. Allen. And the more I thought about her, the more I prayed. But even I was surprised! An hour before the wedding was to begin, the sun came out!

Because Sara and I wanted to be sure to get good seats, we asked my dad to drive us over a little early.

"Sara, you really look cool!" I told her.

"Thanks. I just hope my pantyhose don't fall down!"

Turning in at a white house, we waved to Dad and walked back into a gigantic yard. Our cameras bounced on our chests like awkward necklaces. "Wow! Awesome!" Sara said.

I agreed. Frankly, I didn't know flowers came in so many colors! Two men were setting up folding chairs on the soggy lawn. To the left, three teachers stood under a yellow canopy arranging flowers on tables.

"It's a good thing the rain stopped," Sara said softly. "There's no way that everybody could have fit under that little tent!"

Actually, by coming early, Sara and I got to see everything. As guests began arriving, two ushers brought them down the center and showed them where to sit.

As the kids in my homeroom began to arrive, I acted real cool. Some of the immature boys actually waved. I nearly died when I saw Calvin

Young. If he let out a belch during the wedding, I'd never speak to him again!

When everyone was seated and the music began, I suddenly realized that I was just perching on the front of my folding chair. Oh, no! The back legs were sinking into the wet ground! I looked past Sara down our row of chairs. Everyone was tipping backwards! I hoped we wouldn't all be swallowed up before the ceremony even started!

Actually, I'm not sure where the music was coming from, but I sure didn't see a real orchestra! When an old woman began playing a violin solo, Sara came pretty close to laughing out loud. I had to poke her hard!

And then the wedding march began. As the bride started down the soggy aisle, everyone stood up to watch. I guess Ms. Allen doesn't have a father, because she walked with Sara's teacher, Mr. Campbell. Sara grinned and poked me.

As my teacher came closer, I gasped! I can't even begin to describe how beautiful Ms. Allen looked! Her dress was white, naturally, with little beads on the top and sleeves. The back of the skirt, which dragged across the grass, was getting wet. But nobody seemed to mind!

Mostly I looked at my teacher's face. Mom says all brides are beautiful. Ms. Allen was

41

wearing her special smile—one that always makes me smile too!

"See," Sara whispered. "The groom *is* tall and handsome!"

Of course, Sara was right. Kevin McMann, in a white tuxedo, was standing in front smiling as Ms. Allen walked toward him. He never took his eyes off his bride!

"Isn't it romantic!" Sara whispered. "It's even better than on TV!" That's when I remembered that she had never actually seen a real wedding!

Now everybody sat back down on the folding chairs and waited. At first nothing happened. I glanced around looking for the minister. I couldn't believe it! There didn't seem to *be* a minister!

Finally, a friend of Ms. Allen read a poem about butterflies. I never really got the point.

Next, a woman played a guitar while three men stood in a row and sang about what friends are for. One of the men was Mr. Campbell. Sara grinned and poked me again.

Then a gray-haired man stood up and explained how the bride and groom met. Personally, I think he left out a lot of it! While he spoke, Ms. Allen and Mr. McMann kept looking at each other and smiling.

Now, while the gray-haired man listened, the bride and groom faced each other and made a whole lot of promises. While they put wedding rings on each other's hands, it was very quiet. Afterwards, the gray-haired man told us that they were man and wife.

And then they kissed. Sara squeezed my left hand so hard it hurt. Maybe I imagined it, but I was pretty sure I heard someone giggle!

And then it was over! They were Mr. and Mrs. McMann. Or maybe they were Mr. McMann and Ms. McMann. How should I know?

All along, I kept waiting for somebody to read from the Bible or pray or something. But no one did. This was how I found out you can get married without ever mentioning the name of Jesus!

As the smiling bride and groom started back down the aisle, I glanced at Sara. She actually had tears in her eyes! "Wasn't it romantic?"

"Hey, it's time to take pictures!" I remembered.

"Maybe we can get them to stand in front of the flowers again," Sara said. "That's really our best shot!"

Mr. Campbell must have realized the same thing, because he was trying to get the bride and groom to stand in front again so he could get it on video.

Actually, we got lots of pictures, not only of the happy couple but also the guests. Sara even took a picture of Mr. Campbell taking his videos! And I got one of all the kids in my homeroom.

Afterwards, my teacher motioned for me to come closer. "Kevin, you remember Katie Hooper!"

"I sure do!" He smiled at me. "We're glad you could come! And thanks for taking pictures!"

"It was a great wedding!" I told them.

"Actually, the weather gave us a few gray hairs!" Ms. Allen said, smiling. "But everybody kept assuring me the rain would stop!"

I didn't say anything. I just smiled. "I guess I'd better get some pictures of the food!" I said. "Otherwise, it will be all gone!"

"A good idea!" My teacher smiled. "But, Katie, be sure to take time out for a piece of wedding cake!"

All in all, Sara and I agreed on the way home that it was a wonderful wedding. Guests even got to take home little boxes of special cake for making wishes. "You're supposed to put it under your pillow," Sara told me. "Katie, don't forget!"

"I won't," I said.

But to be honest, I never did make a wish. Because later, when I peeked in at the cake, it looked so good I ate it!

Two Is Company

On the way to Sunday school the next morning, I decided to corner Sara before she cornered me. "Well," I said, "who did you dream about?"

She just looked at me.

"The wedding cake," I said. "Didn't you put it under your pillow and make a wish?"

Sara stared out the car window. "I don't want to talk about it," she said.

Later, as we headed for the church nursery between services, I tried something else. "Sara, today for our Family Day we're going fishing! Dad said I could invite you to come along!"

She didn't hesitate. "I can't," she said.

"Why not?" I was surprised. Sara never has anything to do on Sunday afternoons.

"Mom took the day off. As soon as I get home we're heading for Cripple Creek."

"No kidding!"

Sara made a face. "With Ernie Kennedy!"

"Oh," I said.

On Monday morning, I was just starting to iron when the phone rang. It was for Mom. She hung up the phone and turned to me. "Mrs. Harris called to tell me her wallpaper's in!"

"Good," I said. "Want me to babysit?"

"You read my mind!" Mom grinned. "How about Wednesday?"

"Fine," I said. "Can Sara spend the day here with me?"

"Good idea!" Mom said. "Katie, would you consider inviting Kimberly to join you? Her mother says she's really lonely now that school's out."

"Oh, Mom!" I groaned. "By then the wedding pictures should be ready. Sara and I planned to start organizing them."

"Couldn't it wait a day?"

I shook my head. "Anyhow, you know Kimberly and I don't have anything in common! The time I had her come over after school was a disaster!"

"That was last fall," Mom said. "Things change."

"I'm always nice to Kimberly Harris," I said. "But that doesn't mean I want her for a best

46

friend! Besides, Sara doesn't like her."

"Katie, maybe you and Sara should think about enlarging your circle of friendship!"

I didn't answer. If she made me do it, I would. But Mom didn't say anything else.

When I saw Sara that afternoon, I never even mentioned Mom's idea. Sara looked gloomy enough already. "I take it you didn't have a good time in Cripple Creek?"

"It was all right." Sara forced a smile. "The museum was cool, and the shops were dynamite! Have you ever been there?"

I shook my head. "Maybe we could go next week. It's my turn to plan Family Day."

"You'll like it!" she said.

"But you didn't?"

At first Sara didn't answer. "Katie, I finally figured it out. Ernie Kennedy's after my mother's money!"

"No kidding!" I said. "I didn't know your mother had any money!"

"She doesn't," Sara said. "But at least she has a job."

"What kind of work does Ernie do?"

"He told Mom he's an engineer. The plant where he worked closed down." Sara's eyes got big. "But if that's really true, I don't see why he can't get another job!"

"My father says several plants in Colorado

47

Springs have closed recently," I said. "As a matter of fact, we've been praying for a man at church. He's been out of work for weeks."

"If you promise not to say anything, I'll tell you a secret!" Sara said. She pressed her lips together. "I just don't like him! Mom and I left Omaha so we could start over. And we were doing just fine! We don't need another mouth to feed!"

"You mean Ernie Kennedy eats with you?"

Sara grinned. "Not exactly. Well, he did Saturday night. He brought over a pizza. With everything on it!"

"He came over!" I said. "Is that what was bugging you?"

"It wasn't a big deal," Sara said. "To tell you the truth, we hardly said two words to each other! Mom kept trying to start conversations, but nothing worked. Finally, they went out in his car. And I just stayed home and watched TV."

"Sara, you must have felt left out!"

She shook her head. "Left out! Are you kidding? Do you think I'd miss my favorite programs just to watch those two smile at each other!"

"Well, Sara, at least they took you along to Cripple Creek yesterday," I said.

"They didn't really want me there," she said. "I can tell when I'm not wanted!"

"Maybe you're just sensitive."

"Me, sensitive? Don't make me laugh!"

"Sara," I said, "no offense, but sometimes I think you are!"

"Sure," she said, nodding. "How would you like it if somebody gave you five dollars and told you to meet him back at the car in an hour!"

I took a deep breath. "Sara, do you think your mother would ever get married again?"

"No way!" Sara looked angry. "I'll tell you this for sure! If there's one thing I don't need, it's another father!"

"Tomorrow I'm going up to Flat Rock with my father," I said. "But I'll be here babysitting all day Wednesday. Want to join me? Mom said I could ask you."

"I'd love to!" she said.

I took a breath. "Would you want to include Kimberly Harris?"

"Are you kidding?" Her smile faded. "It's the same old story! 'Two's company; three's a crowd'!"

"Actually, Jesus had lots of friends," I said.

"Sure," Sara remembered. "But some of them were special. Wasn't John His best friend?"

"I guess so," I said.

"Katie, I need you now more than ever!"

I hugged her. "Sara, we'll always be best friends! I promise!"

To be honest, I felt a little guilty on Wednesday morning when Kimberly rode along to pick up Mom. "Hi, Katie," she said. "I saw you taking pictures at the wedding! Wasn't Ms. Allen beautiful?"

"The best," I said, smiling. "I never saw her look so happy!"

"Did you happen to notice the beading on her dress?" Kimberly asked. "Mom and I saw something just like that in *Vogue.*"

"In where?"

"*Vogue,*" Kimberly repeated. "It's a fashion magazine."

"I never heard of it."

"Katie, I have lots of fashion magazines," she said. "Maybe you could come over sometime and look at them with me."

"Sure," I said. I hoped she didn't notice my lack of enthusiasm.

Kimberly spoke faster. "Actually, when I get back from the East, Mom's going to let me try to make one of the outfits for school."

"You know how to sew?" I was surprised.

"I'm learning," Kimberly said, smiling. "Mom's really the expert. She makes almost all my clothes—and her own too. But now she's teaching me all about patterns and stuff."

"No kidding," I said. "By the way, when do you leave for Philadelphia?"

"This weekend. I can hardly wait!"

"I'll call you with my cousin's number."

She smiled. "Wouldn't it be cool if it worked out that I could meet Jennifer Green?"

"It sure would!"

Mrs. Harris was ready to leave. "I could be late," Mom told me. "We'll be having that molded fish salad for supper. You'd better go ahead and feed the baby."

After they left, I couldn't stop thinking about Kimberly. Maybe I should have included her today. Actually, she isn't so bad!

But then when Sara arrived, I could see how much the day meant to her. Shyly, she gave me a big hug! "Hi, Best Friend!" she said.

Wedding, Second Time Around

Looking at our photos of Ms. Allen's wedding was almost as good as being there! I could hardly believe how good the pictures turned out.

Even Sara seemed surprised. "Maybe we really are pros!" she said.

I shook my head. "Maybe we were just lucky!"

"Or maybe the Lord helped us," she said.

I grinned. "Maybe He did!"

Whatever the reason, we ended up with some awesome pictures! Between the two of us, we got shots of everything and everybody. I don't know which were best—those of the bride and groom or those we took of the scene in the back yard.

"In this one, did you realize Calvin Young was making a face?" Sara asked.

I laughed. "No, but I'm not surprised. You know Calvin!"

"Here's a really cool picture of you, Katie!"

I took a good look at it. "That's funny! I don't remember taking that one!"

She giggled. "Of course not, silly! You're in the picture! I took that one!"

I laughed. "My favorite is this one with the bride and groom feeding each other cake!"

She nodded. "Personally, I like the one where she's throwing her bouquet!"

I studied the picture. "Sara, do you think it's true that the woman who caught it will be the next bride?"

"Probably," Sara said. "The rest of the women looked too young or too old!"

"You checked it out?"

"Naturally," Sara said.

I handed her a photo. "What's this one?"

"I don't know," she said, holding it up to the light. Then she grinned. "I might as well admit it. That was supposed to be a shot of the flower garden. Oh, well! Nobody's perfect!"

Actually, sorting all the pictures and putting them in order took longer than we thought. When Mom got home, we still had them spread all over the kitchen table.

"Girls, they're beautiful!" Mom said. "I'm sure Mrs. McMann will be thrilled!"

"But do they look professional?" Sara asked.

Mom laughed. "They're great! As a matter of fact, this one would make a nice enlargement!"

"Tomorrow we'll buy the album," Sara said. "Katie, I'll pick you up at ten o'clock."

After she went home, I turned to Mom. "How did the wallpapering go? Was Mrs. Harris pleased?"

Mom grinned from ear to ear. "It absolutely transformed the dining room!" she said. "To be honest, it's the most expensive paper I've ever hung! Kimberly's mother has excellent taste!"

"Was Kimberly around?" I asked.

"Some," Mom said. "I think mostly she was packing for her trip."

"Right," I said. "She probably wouldn't have had time to come over here anyway."

Mom just looked at me.

"I'll call her tonight with Jennifer's phone number," I said. "Thanks for finding it."

Mom nodded.

To be honest, I felt kind of guilty calling Kimberly. But Sara needs me too! What's a person supposed to do?

"This is Kimberly Harris," said a very cool voice.

"Hi, Kimberly! It's Katie Hooper!" Even as I said it, I knew my voice sounded young—maybe even babyish.

"I bet you have that phone number! Right?" She sounded friendly enough.

"Right!" I said. "Mom also found Jennifer's address."

"Why don't you give me that too!"

Carefully I gave her the information. "I wish I could meet Jennifer," I said. "My mother saw her whole family at my grandfather's funeral. But the rest of us didn't get to go."

"Your mother went to Philadelphia?"

"No. The funeral was in Illinois," I said. "Mom drove all the way by herself!"

"No kidding!" There was this pause. "Katie, is there anything special you want me to tell your cousin?"

I tried to think. "I guess you could tell her I hope she can come to visit me!"

"When?"

Her question took me by surprise. "I don't know," I said. "Just sometime. And maybe you could ask her if she still likes horses."

"She rides? Katie, you didn't tell me she rides!"

"Well, she used to," I said. "And Mom said she even had a boyfriend. I'm curious about him. But that would be too embarrassing, wouldn't it?"

"Probably," Kimberly said. "But maybe it will just come up in the normal conversation. I guess

I could tell her about you and your family. But I don't really know much about them."

"You saw my baby sister when you were here," I reminded her. "And you met my father on the field trip."

"You're right! And don't you have a brother going into high school?"

"His name is Jason," I said. "Ask Jennifer how old her brothers are."

"OK, Katie," Kimberly said. "That gives me some ideas. I'm sure once we get talking I'll think of things to say."

"I'm sure you will," I agreed. One thing Kimberly's very good at is talking.

"I'll call you as soon as I get back," she promised.

"Great! We'll get together!" But after I hung up, in my mind I kept hearing Kimberly's voice ask, "When?"

It took Sara and me three days to arrange the photo album in the right order. At one point, we discovered we had left out the shot of the newlyweds coming back down the aisle. It was murder trying to pull out all the pictures from those little plastic envelopes!

And then the bride and groom weren't back from their honeymoon. Finally a familiar voice answered the phone. "This is Ms. McMann."

"It's me, Katie Hooper!"

"Katie!" she said. "I planned to call you. How did your pictures turn out?"

"I think you'll like them," I told her.

"Oh, good! Can you and Sara bring them over tomorrow afternoon? Come for lemonade!"

"She sounded pretty excited," I told Sara on the way over.

"That's how brides are," Sara explained.

"How do you know?"

She grinned. "I just know," she said.

"Girls, come right in!" Ms. McMann said. "Here, I've poured you some lemonade! Would you like a cookie?"

Sara took two cookies and handed her the imitation leather binder.

Ms. McMann acted like she could hardly wait! Immediately she began looking through the pages. The smile on her face grew bigger and bigger. And then an amazing thing happened. Her eyes filled with tears!

"What's wrong, Ms. McMann?" I asked. It was hard to remember her new name.

"You girls have saved the day!"

We just looked at her.

"The photographer called as soon as we got back," she told us. "Something happened to his film! None of our wedding pictures turned out!"

"No kidding!" Sara said. "And he calls himself a professional!"

"He said nothing like this had ever happened before," Ms. McMann said. "He's giving us our money back. And he's offered to take some poses in his studio. But your pictures are the only photos actually taken on our wedding day!"

"Wow!" I said.

"I'm so grateful!" Ms. McMann said. "I don't want to insult you girls by giving you money. But I'm sure you had expenses like the film and everything. Will this check cover it?"

I glanced down at the check and handed it to Sara. It was the biggest check I've ever seen.

Sara's smile lit up the room. "Please don't worry about insulting us!" she said. "This covers our expenses fine!"

"I'm glad it turned out this way," I told my teacher. "It would be awful for you not to have any wedding pictures at all!"

On the way home, Sara positively danced along beside me. "Katie, now I'm positive that the Lord helped us!" she said.

I just smiled while she carried on about how God launched our professional careers! After all, I realized, Sara just might be right!

We Join the Stampede

In Woodland Park, the biggest deal all year is our Ute Trail Stampede Rodeo. In addition to the rodeo, we have a street dance, a pancake breakfast, a parade, and even a big auto race up Pikes Peak! But even all this wasn't enough to keep Sara's mind off Ernie Kennedy.

"I just don't know what my mother sees in him!" she said.

"Maybe they have fun together," I suggested. "He sure can think up different things to do!"

"We could have thought them up without him!" Sara said.

"But you didn't," I reminded her. "Sara, I've lived in Colorado all my life, and I've never gone to most of the places he's come up with!"

"You're right!" Sara said. "The Air Force Academy. The cog railway. The Flying W Ranch. Royal Gorge. Now he's even talking about taking Mom rafting on the Colorado River! The man really should have been a tour guide!"

"Well, that's an idea!" I said. "Maybe he could get a job as a tour guide!"

Sara shook her head. "He wants to stick with engineering. Even if he has to move away."

"I don't get it," I said. "How could he get a job somewhere else?"

"By writing letters," Sara explained. She smiled for the first time. "Frankly, I'm all for it!"

"How come?"

"Actually, it's probably the best way to get rid of him!" Sara said. "I'm praying he gets a job some place like California!"

"Why don't you like Ernie?" I asked. "Have you figured it out yet?"

"Partly it's the way he looks!" Sara said. "Personally, I like tall men!"

"How about your mother? Does she mind that Ernie's so short?"

"At least Mom's been honest," Sara said. "She admits that his height bothered her at first. But now she says she never thinks about it."

I grinned. "Maybe that will happen to you!"

"Impossible!" Sara said. "Every time I see Mom standing next to that man, I think exactly the same thing. It's ridiculous! That's it, Katie! They look ridiculous!"

"Anyhow, it sure was nice of him to invite me to go to the rodeo with you!" I said.

A funny look came over Sara's face. "You're always sticking up for Ernie Kennedy! But you might as well know, Katie."

"Know what?"

Sara's eyes got big. "I told him I wouldn't even consider going to the rodeo with them unless they took you along too!"

"Oh."

"Anyhow, now that you're coming, I'm starting to get excited about the Stampede Rodeo!" Sara wrinkled up her nose. "Anything that smells that bad must have something going for it!"

I laughed. "It's lots of fun! Even my father goes, and he can't stand horses!"

"Katie, maybe you'd rather go with your family?"

"Are you kidding! This is special! It's my very first time to go to the Stampede with a friend. My best friend!" I added.

"Actually, once we get there, we can pretend we came by ourselves!" Sara said.

"That's not very nice," I scolded. "I mean, Ernie is buying the tickets!"

"Oh, he won't care!" Sara said. "He doesn't

really want me anyhow. I'm sure he just included me so Mom won't feel guilty about leaving me alone all the time!"

But the next day, when I climbed into the back seat of Ernie's car, I noticed that he even remembered my name. "Hi, Katie Hooper!" His smile seemed real enough.

"Hi," I said, sitting next to Sara. "It's sure nice of you to invite me to go with you!"

"We're glad you can make it!" Ernie said. "I know how much Sara likes you!" I watched him glance at Mrs. Wilcox and smile. Sara poked me.

In a little town like ours, parking is always a problem. We had to walk for miles. But as we heard the music coming from the arena, Sara and I started feeling excited. Ahead of us walked the mismatched couple. Sara's right. Mrs. Wilcox and Ernie do make a funny pair!

Our seats were the greatest. Sara wanted to sit on the end, which meant I sat next to Mrs. Wilcox, with Ernie on her other side.

"I hear the stock is tougher than ever," Ernie said, as we waited for the entertainment to begin. "These cowboys follow the good stock around from show to show. That's how they win their money!"

"Mr. Kennedy, did you grow up around horses?" I asked.

Mrs. Wilcox laughed.

He smiled. "Not exactly!" he said. "I grew up in Chicago! But I've been reading up on rodeos! When I live somewhere, I believe in finding out all I can about what's going on there!"

"I'm hungry," Sara said. "Can Katie and I have something to eat?"

"Here you go," Ernie said. He reached across with a ten dollar bill. "Let me know if you need any more!"

"Wow!" I whispered.

"It's a payoff," Sara explained, as we took off to buy refreshments. "Now he can concentrate on impressing my mother!"

When we returned, at first I had a chance to secretly watch the two adults. I noticed that even after the show began, Ernie Kennedy and Mrs. Wilcox seemed more interested in each other than they did in the horses or cowboys!

But once things really got going, I forgot about the adults. The best show was going on down in the arena! Before the day was over, there would be calf roping, bareback riding, and steer wrestling. And bull riding—the most exciting thing of all!

Sara, who had never seen a rodeo before, really got into it. I'm sure she screamed louder than the music, which blared each time the chute opened.

"Wow! I didn't know you could swing a rope so fast!" Sara yelled.

"I remember that cowboy from last year," I hollered. "I think he's the champion!"

"I'm rooting for him!" she said. "This is the greatest!"

"Wait until you see the steer wrestling!" I told her.

But our absolute favorite thing was a cowboy named Slim. Sara and I nicknamed him Yum Yum. Actually, although Sara never did believe it, I knew that Yum Yum is a clown. Whenever a bull rider gets bucked off, Yum Yum tempts the bull to run after him! Then, at the very last minute, he jumps to safety inside a barrel!

"I can't watch!" Sara screamed. "He's pushing his luck!"

I laughed and filled my mouth with popcorn.

"Enjoying the show?" Suddenly I was aware of a man's voice. I turned to see my father standing in the aisle next to Sara.

"Hi, Dad!" I said. "Where are you guys sitting?" Looking where he pointed, I waved to my mother. Although Dad wanted to bring the baby, Mom won out. Today was the first time Amy has ever been left with a non-family babysitter.

"I hear this is your first rodeo, Sara," my father said. "Are you having fun?"

"I sure am, Mr. Hooper!" Sara said. "But I

won't have any voice left by the end!"

Now I realized that Mrs. Wilcox was leaning toward me. "Steve, I'd like to have you meet Ernie Kennedy," she said.

My father smiled and nodded. "My pleasure! Ernie, I hear you're joining us for our Fourth of July picnic!"

"I'm looking forward to it," Ernie said.

"It was so nice of Elizabeth to invite him," Mrs. Wilcox said.

As my father left, he looked down at Sara. "We'll see you in a couple of days!"

"Right!" Sara said. When Dad was gone, she poked me. "You didn't tell me Ernie was invited!"

I swallowed my popcorn. "That's because I didn't know it either," I said.

"It isn't fair! I don't see why he has to horn in on everything we do!"

"What's the difference anyhow?" I asked. "We'll have a good time! Don't forget that Mayblossom McDuff's coming!"

"And Silent Sam?"

I nodded. "The same people who came for Thanksgiving and Christmas. Sara, it's getting to be a tradition! Did you realize you're part of our family? We're like cousins!"

Sara grinned. "If you say so! Did your mom say there's going to be German potato salad?"

"The best you've ever tasted!"

"That settles it! I'm coming!" She smiled.

"Oh, no!" I yelled, looking back at the arena. "Look at Yum Yum! Sara, you're right! He's never going to make it this time!"

We both screamed our heads off. Well, Yum Yum made it! But just in the knick of time!

A Lot to Celebrate!

As you could probably guess, Hoopers aren't a family that celebrates the Fourth of July by shooting off illegal fireworks! Dad thinks fireworks are dangerous. And that's it. Period.

And we didn't really stop to think a lot about our country's independence! Actually, the closest we come to patriotism is putting up our American flag. But this year, because of our move, we didn't have a bracket.

"Elizabeth, can't we just skip it?" Dad asked. "We can celebrate once without the flag."

"You have to be kidding!" Mom was shocked.

"Don't forget, we still have to put up the volleyball net," my brother said.

"It can wait," Mom told him.

"What if the people come?" I asked. "Sara's due any minute."

"Then she can watch," Mom told me. "It just wouldn't be the Fourth of July without the Stars and Stripes!"

"But I don't have a bracket," Dad said. "And the stores aren't open."

Mom smiled. "You'll think of something!"

When Mom gets like this, we all know it's pointless to protest. Personally, I was just glad I wasn't the one responsible for the flag! My job was to set the tables.

The food had been prepared yesterday. Mom always says that the cooking is part of the fun of having a party. She and I made the Jell-O salads in the morning. And after lunch, Sara joined us to help cut up ingredients for Aunt Maurie's German Potato Salad.

"Did I cut it small enough?" Sara asked, showing Mom her celery.

"Perfect!" Mom told her.

"By the way, who is this Aunt Maurie anyhow?" Sara asked.

Mom and I both laughed. "We don't even know her!" I said.

"When I was growing up, she was the aunt of our next-door neighbor," Mom explained. "Of course, my mother made a few changes in her recipe."

"Of course," Sara laughed. "Mrs. Hooper, do you really think I'll get to be a good cook?"

"Why not?" Mom smiled. "Sara, learning to cook is probably easier if you grow up helping in the kitchen. But it's not necessary."

"Besides," I said, "you're getting lots of experience helping us!"

By the time I got the silverware arranged on the picnic tables, my father had worked his way through his entire supply of hardware. "Not one bracket!" he announced.

"How did we hang the flag before?" I asked.

"On a bracket," he said. "But when we moved we left it screwed into the side of the cabin."

"I have an idea," I said. "Let's call Mayblossom. Maybe she could unscrew it and bring it when she comes!"

"I hate to do that," Dad said. "It sounds so stupid."

"She wouldn't care," I said. "But maybe someone else has a bracket."

Suddenly, we both started smiling at the same time. "Sam Johnson!" he said. "Why didn't I think of that before?"

Silent Sam has pulled Dad out of more than one fix. Last winter he saved us from freezing to death by installing a woodburning stove. In my opinion, everyone who lives in an old wreck of a house should know somebody like Silent Sam!

In no time, the white-haired man was climbing out of his truck. "I'm glad you called me!" he said. And you could tell he meant it. "To be honest, I was just hanging around waiting for the time when I could come over here!" he said.

"Here's the pole," Dad told him. "If you can get Old Glory mounted, maybe Elizabeth can settle down and enjoy the day!"

"And then Dad can settle down and enjoy the day too!" I said.

Sam chuckled. "Just give me a minute!" Smiling, he went back to his truck and pulled out a box. "Hmmmmm!" he said, as he poked through the contents. "Let's give this baby a try!"

"Man, you're incredible!" my father said. "Sam, how do you do it?"

Sam laughed. "Experience," he said.

"Hey, I like your flag!" Sara yelled, as she crossed our yard. "Hi, Silent Sam!"

He looked at her and laughed. "Hi, Sara! How's the leading lady?"

"Fine!" Sara was in a good mood. "Mom's coming over in a few minutes. Alone!"

"Is anything wrong?" I asked.

"Beats me," Sara said. "Here, Katie, I'll help you with those plates."

While we finished setting the tables, Dad and Silent Sam helped Jason with the volleyball net. Nobody even noticed when Mayblossom Mc-

71

Duff drove up in her little red sports car. "Hello, everybody!" She waved.

Before I could run over to greet my special friend, Silent Sam took off. "Wait there, Mayblossom!" he told her. "I'll carry your things." As she watched him take his huge steps toward her, a smile spread across the author's face.

The sound of voices brought Mom to the kitchen door. "Welcome, everybody!" she said. When she stepped onto the porch, my dog came along.

"Elizabeth, come out here and see your flag!" Dad said. "Sam saved the day!"

"It looks great!" Mom looked happy. "Now it finally feels like the Fourth of July!"

Suddenly, January stood with his nose in the air and began to howl. *AaaaOooooo!*

"Quit it!" I told him. "What's wrong? They aren't strangers! You know these people!"

AaaaaaOooooo! The stupid dog howled again. *AaaaaOooooo!*

Mayblossom began to laugh. "Don't stop him, Katie! Let him sing!" she said. "He's finally performing the 'Star Spangled Banner' on the right day!"

Well, maybe I do have a patriotic dog. Or maybe January just spotted Sara's mother heading up the sidewalk. "Hi," Mrs. Wilcox said. "Happy Fourth of July!"

"Same to you!" Dad said. "Is Ernie sick?"

"No, I'm the one with a cold," Mrs. Wilcox said. "Ernie's fine! He just had to wait for a telephone call."

Next, a tall boy jumped out of a car and walked toward us. Sara poked me. "Wow! Who's that?"

"It's Peter, one of Jason's friends from church," I whispered.

Sara grinned. All during the introductions she grinned. But neither Peter nor my brother seemed to notice. "Tell us when the food's ready!" Jason said. "We're going to pitch horse-shoes."

"Katie, I brought you and Sara a surprise!" Smiling, Mayblossom waved it in the air.

"Your new book! It's finally out!" I ran over to hug her.

Sara joined me. "Me too!" she said.

And then an amazing thing happened. Grinning from ear to ear, Silent Sam got in line behind Sara. "Me too!" he laughed.

Mayblossom's face got red. "Sam Johnson! What will people think?"

"Mayblossom, they're our friends," Sam said softly. "I think we'll have to tell them sooner or later!" I noticed the way he smiled at her. I had seen that look before. It reminded me of the way Dad sometimes looks at my mother.

"Hey, you two!" Mom said. "What's going on?"

Mayblossom glanced at Sam. Then her eyes twinkled and a smile filled her entire face. "Oh, why not?" she said. "Last night this dear man asked me to marry him!"

Sara and I squealed.

Mom rushed over to hug Mayblossom. My father grabbed Sam's hand. "You old fox, you! And we called you Silent Sam!"

Sam smiled. "Well, she still hasn't said 'yes'!" But everybody in the yard could tell what her answer was going to be!

Then, just as things were settling down a little, Ernie Kennedy came across the yard. He looked happier than I had ever seen him. "Good news!" he said. "I got my phone call. I have a job interview in New Jersey!"

And then I saw that look *again!* This time it was the way Ernie smiled at Sara's mother. Like she was the only person in the yard.

Suddenly, it dawned on me. It was exactly the way the groom had looked at the wedding, as he watched my teacher come down the aisle!

Wow! I wondered if Sara had noticed. But Sara's mind was not on her mother. No, she was too busy watching Peter and Jason pitch horseshoes!

"Let's bring out the food!" Mom said. "This calls for a celebration!"

Another Proposal

Well, it probably would have been an unforgettable picnic even without Aunt Maurie's German Potato Salad! Never in my entire life have I seen so much smiling!

"Mayblossom McDuff, what a surprise!" Mom said, as we finished eating. "Here we pictured you enjoying the rest of your life alone up there in your mountain cabin!"

The writer smiled. "Actually, that was my plan! Honestly, I never dreamed that at my age romance would find its way into my story!"

Dad laughed. "What do you mean 'at your age'? When it comes to enjoying life, you're more fun that most kids!"

"So you noticed it too!" Sam laughed. But then

he got serious. "Can I tell you something? When my wife died, the light went out in my life! Seeing all the love here in the Hooper family only made me feel lonelier! But then you invited M. and me to share your Thanksgiving! Well, that was the beginning!"

"I think that's when you started to talk more," I remembered. "Now I may have to think up a new nickname!" Everybody laughed.

"How about you, Mayblossom?" Sara's mother asked. "Was it love at first sight?"

Mayblossom laughed her tinkling little laugh. "Not exactly! To be honest, I thought Sam Johnson was the quietest man I ever met!" She smiled at him. "Quiet, but awfully nice!"

"Actually, I liked her independence!" Sam said. "Lots of women would be miserable all alone in a mountain cabin! But Mayblossom thought it was wonderful!"

"It is wonderful!" Mayblossom said. "But now I realize that sharing things with Sam is pretty wonderful too! I'll tell you what really attracted me to him. I've never known a man with a greater love for the Lord!"

"Hey, everybody, are you sure you don't want something else to eat?" Mom asked. "How about you, Ernie?"

"I'm stuffed!" He grinned. "Believe me, this is one Fourth of July I'll never forget!"

The next morning Sara and I were still talking about Mayblossom and Silent Sam.

"The amazing thing is that they're perfect together!" I told Sara. "And I never even realized it!"

"That's how romances work!" Sara said.

"Personally, I think the Lord did it!" I told her. "First, He gave Mayblossom a great life alone. And now she's getting married besides!"

Sara grinned. "I just hope the Lord doesn't make me wait so long!"

"Mom says Jesus always gives us what's best if we trust Him!"

"Your mother's right, Katie!" Sara smiled. "Remember when I hoped He'd send Ernie Kennedy to California? Well, New Jersey's even better!"

"Sara, Ernie doesn't have the job yet!" I said.

"True." She smiled. "But I just know the Lord will take that man out of our lives!"

Personally, I wasn't so sure. But I didn't say anything. I'm finally learning that I don't always know exactly what the Lord has in mind!

Suddenly, Sara looked up from her quilt. "Oh, no! What time is it?" she asked. "Mom left me a note. She's coming home to have lunch with me. I wonder what's up."

"Can you come back afterwards?" I asked. "Sewing is lots more fun when we do it together!"

"Sure!" She smiled. "See ya!"

But Sara didn't come back. Finally, I decided if she didn't come out by two o'clock, I'd call her. At ten minutes before two, I looked out the door and saw Sara walking slowly toward my house. As she came closer, I could see she was crying.

"What's wrong, Sara?" I asked.

"We should never have come to the picnic!" she sobbed.

"Sara, sit down," I said. "Try to calm down. I'll get you a Kleenex."

As I entered the kitchen, Mom asked, "What's wrong?"

"I don't know. Sara's crying!"

"Oh, my!" Mom said. "I'm going upstairs to leave you two alone. Katie, I know you'll handle it! You're a wonderful friend!" I hoped she was right.

Finally, Sara dried her tears. I've never seen her look so unhappy. She blew her nose. "If we hadn't come to the picnic, it never would have happened!" she said.

"What wouldn't have happened?" I asked.

"It was all that talk about romance," Sara said. "It's all Silent Sam's fault!"

"What did he do?" I asked.

Sara's eyes got big. "You know! He asked Mayblossom McDuff to marry him, that's what!"

"So? I don't get it!"

79

"I'm sure that's what gave Ernie Kennedy the idea!" Sara said.

Suddenly, I caught on. "It sounds like something happened after you got home. Right?"

"I should have known something was up when Mom sent me to bed!" Sara said. "She never sends me to bed!"

I just waited.

Tears filled Sara's eyes again. "Katie, last night Ernie Kennedy asked my mother to marry him!"

I took a deep breath. "Wow! No kidding! Is she going to do it?"

"I think she wants to," Sara said. "Mom says she really loves Ernie. But she doesn't want me to be unhappy!"

"Oh, my!" I said.

"The trouble is, I am unhappy! Katie, I've never been so unhappy in my life!"

"Do you know exactly why?" I asked.

"Sure," she said. "I just don't like him! You know that! And the feeling's mutual! Ernie doesn't like me either!"

"Would your mother marry him anyway?"

"I don't know," Sara said. "I hope not!"

I thought of something. "But if you spoil it for them, then your mother will be unhappy!" I said. "Sara, you don't want that, do you?"

"I was here first!"

"You didn't answer my question," I said. "Sara, you don't want your mother to be unhappy, do you?"

"Of course not. But why couldn't she find some other way to get happy?"

I shook my head. "I don't know, Sara. I think this problem is too big for either of us! Maybe we'd better stop trying to figure it out and just pray about it!"

"It's no use!" Sara said. "Mom doesn't know a thing about Jesus or the Bible! And I doubt if Ernie does either!"

"So? That won't stop the Lord from answering your prayer!"

We just sat there for a minute. "Well, there's one good thing anyway," Sara said. "Ernie invited me to go with them to Denver on Friday."

"Wow!" I said.

Sara's eyes brightened. "Katie, there's this place called Elitch Gardens. It's an amusement park!"

"No kidding!"

"But that isn't the greatest thing, Katie. Mom says there's a theater right in the park. And Ernie got us tickets to a Broadway play!"

"Really?"

"Really! I can't believe it! I'm finally going to see my first real professional tour company!" Sara smiled. She probably couldn't help it.

"Sara, that's wonderful!" I said. "See! Ernie can't be all bad!"

"Oh, I don't know! I'm afraid it's the same old story!" Sara said. "Ernie invites me so Mom won't feel guilty! Only now it isn't just a Saturday evening, Katie! The man wants to marry my mother!"

"I still think we should pray," I said.

"All right, you win," Sara said. She bowed her head.

I closed my eyes. "Lord," I prayed, "You're the only one who can sort this out! You're the God of love so You must want everybody to be happy! Please work it out! Amen."

I waited. Finally, I heard Sara's voice. She was crying again. "Lord, please help me! I'm so scared! If Mom loves Ernie, what's going to happen to me? I need somebody to love me! Besides You, I mean!"

Now Sara was silent. I nearly opened my eyes. But suddenly she thought of something else. "If Ernie Kennedy really likes me, then prove it!"

Afterwards, I put my arms around her. "I love you, Sara!" I said softly. "I'll always love you! I promise!"

Mrs. Wilcox Gets Sick

When it comes to praying, Sara and I have always been different. It might take her a while to do it, but once Sara turns something over to the Lord, she figures it's His problem!

The next day, you'd never guess Sara had been upset! We spent all morning at her house polishing Mrs. Wilcox's silver. Considering how black it was, the two dollars we'd each receive was a bargain. Sara's mom was still trying to get over her cold, so we were trying to work quietly while she rested in her room.

Finally, I was so curious I couldn't stand it any longer. "Has your mother said anything more about marrying Ernie?" I asked.

Sara shook her head. "She's been too busy

blowing her nose! And personally, I've stopped worrying about it!"

"Tell me about Ernie's interview," I said. "What kind of job is it?"

"Beats me!" Sara said. "I think Mom called it research management."

"Wow!" I said. "I'm impressed!"

"Katie, most jobs *sound* important," Sara told me. "For example, nobody collects garbage anymore. Now garbage men are all called waste engineers!"

"Oh."

"Besides, Ernie thinks his old plant might open up again anyhow." She made a face.

I decided to change the subject. "Have you decided what you're wearing to Denver on Friday?"

"Now that's a problem!" Sara smiled. "I can't decide whether to dress for the amusement park or the theater!"

"What's the difference?"

"Are you kidding?" Sara said. "I could hardly wear pantyhose going down a water slide in a log boat!"

"Who said anything about pantyhose?"

"I did," Sara said. "And whoever heard of wearing a tee shirt to the theater!"

I laughed. "So take a suitcase!"

"Sure," Sara said.

"You'll think of something!" I said. I sounded just like my mother.

"I wonder if we'll see *Phantom of the Opera?*" Sara said.

"What are you talking about?"

"It's a play!" Sara smiled. "Katie, didn't I tell you we're going to see a Broadway play?"

"I know what a play is," I said slowly. "But exactly what is a *Broadway* play?"

"You mean you haven't heard of Broadway?" Sara's eyes got big. "Broadway really means New York! Actually, they say it's magical! Don't you know that Broadway's where they have the best plays in the entire world?"

Well, I hate to feel stupid. "But what about television?" I asked. "Or Hollywood? Sara, I always thought you wanted to be a movie star!"

Sara shook her head. "Oh, movies are OK," she said, getting a faraway look in her eyes. "But for an actress, Broadway is where it's at! Broadway is what we all dream about!"

"But if Broadway's in New York, how can you see it in Denver?" I asked.

"I'm not exactly sure," Sara admitted. "But maybe they have a deal with Elitch Gardens or something."

"Well, no wonder you're excited!" I said.

She smiled from ear to ear. "Actually, Katie, Friday is going to be the best day of my life!"

The next afternoon we decided to check out the sales at Ben Franklin. Well, to be honest, there weren't exactly any sales. Sara wanted to check out the lipstick.

"Don't worry! Mom won't even notice!" Sara said. "She'll be too busy smiling at Ernie Kennedy."

"But won't you feel funny?" I asked. "Most girls our age don't wear lipstick, do they?"

"Maybe not most girls," Sara said, tossing her head. "But all actresses do! And I need to be prepared. Somewhere in the audience there might be a talent scout!"

"How would he find you?" I asked.

"They have their ways," Sara told me.

Personally, I thought the lipstick would clash with her red hair, but then I've never really been into drama.

"Let's stop in at the restaurant," Sara said. "But, Katie, you've got to promise you won't tell my mother about the lipstick!"

"I won't tell her," I said. "Besides, she'll probably be too busy smiling at Ernie Kennedy."

"Ernie won't be there," Sara told me.

"Has he stopped drinking coffee?" I asked.

Sara laughed. "No, silly! He's gone to New Jersey for his interview!"

But when we walked into the restaurant, a man wearing an apron greeted us. "Hi, Sara!"

"Hi, Tom!" she said. "Where's Mom?"

"She went home sick," the cook said. "Her temp was over 101! I told her she should be in bed! Besides, there's no business anyhow!"

"My mother wasn't sick this morning."

"You know she's had that cold all week," Tom said. "Now it's gone down into her chest. I'm no doctor, but I think she has bronchitis!"

"Let's go, Katie." Sara turned and held the door.

"Do you have a doctor?" I asked.

"I don't think so," she said. "Katie, she's never been sick. If anything happens to my mother, I don't know what I'll do!"

"Don't worry," I told her. "Once Jason had bronchitis. It isn't real serious."

"There isn't even a hospital in this two-bit town!" Sara said. "We should have stayed in Omaha!"

"Quit it, Sara!" I said. "You're just being dramatic! I'm sure whatever your mother has can be fixed with a shot or something!"

"Well, OK," she said. "But if she dies and I'm left an orphan, can I live with you?"

"Of course," I said. "In the meantime, I bet my mother will know what to do!"

When we got to my house, Dad was already waiting for us. "Where have you girls been?" he asked. "Sara, your mother is sick!"

"I know," Sara said.

"How did you find out, Dad?" I asked.

"Mrs. Wilcox called from the restaurant to see if Sara was here," he said. "When Mom heard what was wrong, she left to pick her up. I think she planned to take her to the doctor."

"Mr. Hooper, if I become an orphan, is it OK if I live with you?" Sara asked.

Dad winked. "Sure!" he said. "After all, Sara, you practically live here anyway!"

"Dad!" I said. "I told Sara bronchitis isn't serious!"

My father grinned. "Can you girls take care of Amy? I was right in the middle of a sketch."

"I'll get her!" I said, picking up the whining baby. I handed Amy a teething biscuit and took her outdoors to her stroller.

"Maybe I should go get my pajamas," Sara said. "Do you think I'll have to sleep over?"

"Maybe," I said. "Hey, Sara, maybe we could take our sleeping bags up into the turret!"

"No way!" Sara said, grinning. "I still think it's haunted!"

"Here they come!" I said. You can spot Purple Jeep a mile away! I carried Amy, and we ran out to the curb to meet our mothers.

"We're all set!" Mom told us. "We just have to put our invalid to bed. Sara, maybe you'd better ride along with us."

"Mom, are you OK?" Sara asked.

Frankly, Mrs. Wilcox didn't look so great. "My cold has turned into bronchitis," she said in a hoarse voice. "The doctor gave me a shot."

"You'll be OK, won't you, Mom?" Sara asked. "I've really been worried!"

"I'll be fine in a few days." Mrs. Wilcox smiled. "But the doctor wants me to stay in bed."

"Then I'll take care of you!" Sara said. "And Katie can help me. We'll even make you soup and Jell-O!"

"That's nice!" Mrs. Wilcox said. "But, Sara, I'm afraid I have some bad news. The doctor said I can't possibly go up to Denver on Friday. I'm afraid our trip to Elitch Gardens will have to be cancelled."

Sara's Surprises

Sara Wilcox really surprised me. I knew how much she was looking forward to going to that Broadway play. So I thought for sure she'd blame her mother for ruining her life. Instead, she devoted the next two days to taking care of her!

"I can't just leave Mom here alone!" she told me. "What if she needs something?"

"Like what?" I asked.

"Like a glass of water! Or a bowl of soup!"

"Sara, if you don't ease up, your mother will float away!" I told her.

"You really surprise me, Katie Hooper!" she said. "I always thought you were more kind and compassionate!"

"But your mother's getting better!" I said. "You told me yourself that her temp is down. And she isn't coughing nearly as much!"

"I still think Mom needs me!" Sara said. "And besides, I need her! When I heard she was sick, I realized how much I love her!"

Well, naturally I was glad! But to be honest, I looked forward to hanging out at my house again. I guess I'm just not used to so much neatness!

On Thursday afternoon, while Mrs. Wilcox was taking a nap, the telephone rang. Since I was right there, I couldn't help listening in.

"Oh, hi!" Sara said. "When did you get back?"

(I knew it had to be Ernie Kennedy!)

"Oh, she's a lot better!" Sara said. "I've kept her in bed just like the doctor said. Her temp's down. And she isn't coughing as much!"

(It sounded like he knew Mrs. Wilcox was sick!)

"But Mom told me the plans were off! She said we aren't going to Denver!" Sara said.

(You mean, they are?)

"Well, sure!" Now Sara's eyes were getting big. "Of course I'd still like to go with you!" She was starting to smile. "Well, you're probably right. I guess she'll be OK here without me!"

(Wow! He was going to take Sara!)

"No kidding!" A huge smile spread across

Sara's face. "Oh, I don't know exactly when it started, Ernie. You might say that I've always had an interest in drama!"

(I've never seen Sara look so happy!)

"Well, she's not really into Broadway theater," Sara said. "But I could ask her. Actually, she's standing right here!"

(Oh? They were talking about me!)

"Ten o'clock? I'll be ready by nine-thirty!" Sara was almost dancing up and down. "And Ernie! Thanks a lot!"

"Wheeee!" Sara hung up the phone and twirled around in total delight!

"What's up?" I asked, pretending I was too dumb to figure it out.

"It's still on!" Sara said. "Ernie's still going to take me to the Broadway play!" She was grinning from ear to ear. "And you know what? He planned the trip to Denver especially for me! Somehow he found out I'm interested in acting!"

"Wow!" I said. "That was nice!"

"Nice?" Sara said. "I've never felt so special in my entire life! Ernie said it's too bad Mom can't come. But since taking me was really the main point, he never even considered cancelling the plans!"

That's when Mrs. Wilcox appeared in her bathrobe. "What's happening?" she asked.

Sara ran over and hugged her mother. "Ernie's

taking me to Denver!" she said. "He's taking me anyway!"

Sara's mother was smiling. "Really?"

"You already knew, didn't you?" Sara asked. "Mom, I hope you don't feel left out! Are you sure you'll be all right here alone?"

"I'll be fine!" her mother said. She grinned. "Actually, it will give me a good rest!"

"Oh, Katie, I almost forgot!" Sara turned to me. "Ernie asked if you can use the extra ticket?"

Me? I'd have to get a substitute for my baby-sitting job. And then I remembered the rodeo. "Sara, even if I can't make it, you'll still go any-way, won't you?"

"Are you kidding, Katie?" Sara grinned. "Are you out of your mind?"

Well, Friday was Sara's day, all right. Sara's and Ernie's. Actually, I might as well not have even been there! Oh, I didn't mind too much. Since I've never been to Denver, I was almost as excited as Sara. Plus it was special just to see Sara so happy!

When they picked me up Friday morning, Sara was already sitting in the front next to Ernie. So I sat in the back seat alone. All the way to Denver I looked out the window and lis-tened to them talk. Mostly they talked about Broadway.

"I can't believe you've seen all those plays!" Sara told him. "You even saw *Les Mis!*"

"It was the best!" Ernie said. "At the end, the whole audience stood up and cheered!"

Actually, Sara didn't ignore me totally. Once in a while, she'd turn around and say something like, "Did you hear that, Katie!" I'd just smile and say something like, "Wow!" Mostly, however, they seemed to forget I was even there.

As we saw the tall buildings of Denver up ahead, Sara was still at it. "Tell me again about *Annie!*" she said. "Ernie, be honest! Do you really think I'd be perfect for the part?"

To be honest, the day in Denver was almost too much for me! I mean, I've hardly been anywhere. And now there was so much to see and remember that I felt overwhelmed.

"Isn't this cool?" Sara said, as we left our car and strolled around the grounds of the park. "I had no idea there would be flowers!"

"That's probably why they call it Elitch Gardens," I said.

Ernie laughed real hard. "That's a good one, Katie!"

Even I knew it wasn't that funny! But it was fun to feel that for once I was fitting in.

"I'm going to let you girls enjoy the rides," Ernie said. "Frankly, I'm just as glad to get out of riding the roller coaster!"

I soon found out what he meant. I've never screamed so loud in my life! And Sara's scream was even louder than the time when we were crawling in our secret passageway!

But afterwards, she really surprised me. "Let's do it again!" she said.

"You have to be kidding, Sara!" I said.

She turned to Ernie Kennedy. "OK. Ernie, will you take me this time?" Reluctantly, he agreed. And they went off, hand in hand.

Well, you get the picture. It was always the same. "But, Ernie, we need you to show us how to play miniature golf!" Sara said.... "But, Ernie, if you don't ride on the log boat with us, you'll miss seeing the old logging operations!"

Later, although Ernie encouraged us to order anything on the menu, I quickly decided on a hamburger. I certainly didn't want anyone to know I'd never heard of most of the other things!

But Sara didn't mind. "What's this one?" Sara asked Ernie. "Do you think I'll like it?" Naturally, Sara liked it. Then afterwards, we all got big ice cream sundaes.

By the time we finished eating and found our seats in the theater, I knew I was tired. But what happened was so embarrassing that if I thought Sara or Ernie knew, I'd die!

To be honest, I kept falling asleep! I'd watch for a few minutes, and then I could feel my head nodding! Sometimes the music woke me up again. Other times I was awakened by loud clapping! When I wasn't napping, I tried to look excited so Ernie and Sara wouldn't catch on.

"Katie! Want to get a Coke?" As the lights went on for the intermission, I saw Sara looking at me funny.

"I'd love to," I said. "Actually, I could use a little walk."

Sara smiled. "We'll be right back, Ernie!"

Ernie smiled back. "I'll be here!"

I followed Sara and the rest of the crowd up the aisle. Frankly, I don't think she ever intended to stop for a Coke. The line at the washroom was the longest I've ever seen!

"Well?" she said, as we waited. "What do you think?"

I faked it. I had no other choice. "It's really cool!" I said. "You were right, Sara. I'll never forget my first Broadway play!"

Sara grinned. "Not the play, Katie! Isn't Ernie Kennedy wonderful!"

Sara Shares
Her News

"Girls, it's been a long day." Ernie smiled as we walked back to the car. "I hope you'll be able to sleep on the way home."

It sounded good to me! But Sara had another idea. "Katie, you can sleep in the back seat. But if you don't mind, Ernie, I'll just sit up here and keep you company!"

Well, that did it! I'm no baby! I decided I'd stay awake too! I sat up straight in the back seat and tried to think of something to say.

However, in spite of my earlier naps, my eyes simply would not stay open. Once we left Denver, there was nothing to look at. Gradually, the voices in the front seat began to fade.

I must have slept quite a while, because when

I woke up, we were in a city. It had to be Colorado Springs. Not that I recognized it. But it's the only city on the way home.

Suddenly, I heard Sara's voice in the front seat. "Ernie, I have a question," she said.

"Hey, Sara, you woke up!" Ernie said. "You had a nice little rest, didn't you?"

"I guess so," she said. There was a pause. "Ernie, are you and my mother really going to get married?"

At first Ernie didn't answer. "Your mother and I have grown to love each other very much!" he said. "Sara, she's a very special lady!"

"I know," Sara said. "And I don't ever want her to get hurt or anything!"

"I don't either!" Ernie said. "I promise I'll never hurt her! I've searched all my life to find the woman I love. And I intend to spend the rest of my life making her happy!"

"I never knew my real father," Sara said. "He died when I was little."

"He must have been a good man," Ernie said. "He certainly has a beautiful daughter!"

"He had red hair too!" Sara said. "In fact, that's probably where my red hair came from!"

Ernie laughed. "No kidding!"

"I guess that was a stupid thing to say, wasn't it?"

"Of course not, Sara," he said. "I wasn't making fun of you! I guess you aren't used to being teased."

"I guess not."

"Sara, teasing doesn't have to hurt people," Ernie said. "I only kid people I like a lot!"

"Like Mom?"

"Like your mom," he said. "And you!"

"Does that mean you like me a lot too?"

"I do like you a lot, Sara! Actually, I'm kind of glad your mother didn't come with us today! I feel like I've had a chance to really get to know you. And I think you're terrific!"

"Really?" There was a pause. "Ernie, will you promise you won't feel bad if I tell you something?"

"I promise."

"I didn't used to like you."

"That's what I figured," Ernie said. "If I hadn't loved your mother so much, I probably would have given up long ago!"

"I'm glad you didn't give up!" Sara said. "I don't exactly know what happened, but now I like you a lot!"

"You do? Why, Sara Wilcox! If I weren't driving through the middle of Colorado Springs, I'd stop the car right now and hug you! Does this mean you're in favor of the marriage?"

"I guess so!" Sara said. "In fact, I hope you two do get married! Want me to tell Mom?"

"What if we both told her?" Ernie suggested. "Do you think her temp will go back up if we wake her when we get to your house?"

Sara laughed. It was a laugh of pure joy! "She'll be so surprised I bet she'll faint!"

Well, I guess Ernie couldn't stand it any longer. He let out a loud "Yahoo!"

I saw Sara turn around. "Hey, hold it down, Ernie!" she giggled. "You'll wake Katie!"

"This is my lucky day!" Ernie said. "Now all I need is a job!"

"You'll find one!" Sara said. "I know you will!"

Now the car was silent. As we headed up Ute Pass, I think I was just starting to doze off again. And then Sara spoke. "Ernie," she said, "can I ask you something very personal?"

"Sure." Ernie chuckled. "Of course, I may not answer you!"

Sara giggled. "This is kind of embarrassing. But here goes! After you and Mom get married, do you think I could call you Dad?"

"Sara, I'd be honored to have you call me Dad!" he said. "A terrific kid like you!" And then he let out another loud "Yahoo!"

"Hey, what's going on up there?" I asked.

"Oh, Ernie, now you did it! You woke Katie!" she said, turning around in her seat.

"He sounds happy," I said. "Is there a reason?"

"I've got some exciting news!" Sara said. "Katie, I'll tell you all about it in the morning!"

When we got to my house, Ernie walked me up to the back door. My father was waiting for me in his bathrobe. "Hi, Ernie!" he said. "I'll bet you're exhausted!"

"Not really!" Ernie said. "As a matter of fact, Steve, I've never felt more wide awake in my whole life!"

The next morning, I didn't say a word about what I had overheard. It was Sara's news, and I wanted her to have the fun of telling it. I hung around the kitchen after breakfast waiting for her to call. But the phone never rang.

"Sara's probably sleeping in," Mom said. "Katie, I'm surprised you're up so early."

"I'm too excited," I told her. "After all, it was my first time in Denver!"

"It sounds wonderful," Mom said. "Maybe we could go up to Elitch Gardens for a Family Day! What do you think, Katie?"

"Sure! If we held Amy, she could ride on the merry-go-round," I said. "We could take a picnic. And if we skipped the play, it wouldn't be so expensive."

Suddenly the telephone rang. I leaped to get it. "Katie!" said a familiar voice. "It's Kimberly. Kimberly Harris."

"Oh," I said. "Hi, Kimberly. When did you get back? Did you talk to my cousin?"

"I got back last night," she said. "Could you come over this afternoon? I can't wait to tell you all about it."

"Don't keep me in suspense!" I said. "Did you talk to Jennifer Green?"

"Well, not exactly."

"Oh." I can't tell you how disappointed I felt.

"So, can you ask your mother?" she said.

"Ask her what?"

"If you can come over!" Kimberly said. "If you need a ride, my mother will pick you up!"

"To be honest, Kimberly, I kind of have other plans for today," I told her. "How about if I call you back?"

"That didn't sound very nice, Katie!" Mom said, after I hung up. "I gather she didn't talk to Jennifer."

"I can't spend the afternoon at Kimberly's!" I said. "I happen to know that Sara has something exciting going on!"

"She's coming over?" Mom asked.

"I wouldn't be a bit surprised!" I said. "I think I'll call and find out when!" But the line was busy.

"Well, you might as well get started on your chores," Mom said.

It was almost lunch time when Sara flew up our back stairs and called through the screen door. "Katie! Katie Hooper!"

"She's right here, Sara," Mom laughed.

"Stick around, Mrs. Hooper!" Sara said. "You'll want to hear this too!"

I smiled. "Well, Sara, what's up?"

Sara was too excited to sit down. "They're getting married! Mom and Ernie Kennedy! And I'm going to be the bridesmaid!" She stopped to take a breath.

"Wow!" I said.

"That's wonderful news, Sara!" Mom told her. "You certainly seem happy about it!"

"If you think *I'm* happy, you should see my mother and Ernie!" Sara laughed. "Personally, I'm thrilled to be getting a father of my own! And what a guy! He sure was worth waiting for!"

Smiling, I thought, "Thank You, Lord!"

"Well," Mom said, "have they set a date for the wedding?"

"Not exactly," Sara said. "But it won't be long!" She grinned. "I have something else to tell you! Ernie found out this morning that he's got a new job! In research planning management!"

"Wow! Sara, that's wonderful!" I said.

"So I'll be moving!" Sara said. "We're going to move to New Jersey!"

I was shocked. I just stood there and looked at Sara. I couldn't say a word.

Some Dreams Come True

Maybe I should have seen it coming. But the fact is, I didn't! Ever since Sara Wilcox came into my life almost a year ago, we've been best friends. And now I was losing her!

"What's wrong, Katie?" Sara asked. "I thought you'd be happy for me!"

"I am, Sara," I said. "But I never figured you'd be moving away!"

She grinned. "Me either! And especially not to New Jersey!"

"But we'll never see each other again!"

"Don't be silly, Katie!" she said. "I'll visit you. And you can come to visit me! And in between times, we can write letters!"

"I guess so," I said.

"Ernie's going to fly out on Monday to find us a place to live," she said. "Mom wants to be settled so I can start middle school out there."

"Actually, it's probably the perfect time to move," Mom told her. "All the other kids will be starting to make new friends too."

"Thanks for telling me that, Mrs. Hooper!" Sara smiled at Mom.

"Just exactly where is New Jersey anyhow?" I asked.

"I looked it up," Sara said. "It's right on the Atlantic Ocean. In the encyclopedia, it says they have wonderful sandy beaches! I may learn to swim yet!"

"That's really far away," I said. "How can you take your furniture?"

"In a huge moving van," Sara said. "Ernie's going to get one big enough for all our stuff, plus everything at his apartment!"

"It's good you were just renting your house here," Mom said. "Selling a house takes a long time!"

"We won't miss this one," Sara said. "To tell the truth, Mom never did like the kitchen wallpaper! Ernie says now she can choose whatever she wants!"

They seemed to have thought of everything. "Where will they have the wedding?" I asked.

Sara shook her head. "I suggested finding a

garden. But Mom didn't go for it."

Suddenly I had an idea. "Sara, maybe we can take wedding pictures again!"

"Maybe you can, Katie," Sara said. "I'll mention it to Mom. But didn't I tell you I'm going to be in it? I even get to pick out my bridesmaid dress. What would you think of one in royal blue!"

"With your hair that would be lovely!" Mom told her.

I agreed. "Hey, Sara, want to stay for lunch?"

"Sorry, I can't," she said, looking at her watch. "I'd better get going! Ernie's cooking something special! We're celebrating!"

"You mean he knows how to cook?" I asked.

Sara grinned. "Another lucky break!" She laughed. "But don't worry, Mrs. Hooper! I'll never forget all you've taught me!"

Then Sara went home and there was—nothing! Home Sweet Home was absolutely quiet. Slowly, I stood up. "I'll see you later, Mom! I think I'll go up to my room."

I closed my door behind me and stood there motionless. I couldn't think of a single thing I wanted to do. Suddenly, I realized how tired I was. I curled up on my bed and went to sleep.

By the time I woke up, the rest of my family had already finished lunch. I sat alone at the kitchen table eating a peanut butter sandwich.

"Mom, I can't remember. Did Sara say she was busy this afternoon?"

"I don't think so," my mother said. "But, Katie, why don't you call Kimberly Harris?"

"Oh, Mother!" I said. I hardly ever call her that. "I'm going to Sara's! See ya!"

But at Sara's, nobody was home. The draperies were pulled shut. I turned to go back.

I looked up Kimberly's number and dialed. The phone rang and rang. Finally I gave up.

As soon as I hung up, our phone starting ringing. Maybe it was Sara! Smiling, I grabbed the telephone.

"Katie, it's Mrs. Stone," said the voice. "I know it's last minute. But is there any chance you could babysit tonight?"

I knew I wasn't doing anything. "Just a minute. I'll ask Mom."

"As long as it won't be late," Mom said. "Tomorrow's Sunday, you know!"

To be totally honest, babysitting's not always as much fun as it was at first! But at least it was something to do. And once I got there, I knew I'd enjoy seeing the children. And the dog!

The next morning, on the way to church, Sara was still bubbling. "I just can't wait to tell Mayblossom McDuff!" she said.

Actually, I hated myself for thinking it. But I couldn't help it. *Once Sara's gone, at least I won't have to share Mayblossom any longer!*

"Hey, what are you thinking?" Sara asked.

"Nothing," I said. "It's too bad we never got to be in the same Sunday-school class."

"I'll have to find a new Sunday school in New Jersey," Sara realized. "I wonder how I'll do that?"

"You'll find a way," I told her.

After Sunday school, on the way to the church nursery, Sara was even more excited. "Wait until you hear this, Katie!"

"Now what?"

"Mayblossom couldn't believe it!" Sara said. "She used to live in Morristown."

"So?"

"Morristown is in New Jersey!" Sara said. "M. still has lots of friends there!"

"So what?" I said. "They'll be too old for you, Sara!"

"I know that! What's wrong with you today?"

"I don't know," I said. "I guess I'm tired or something."

"Guess what we're doing this afternoon?" Sara said.

"I give up!"

"We're going to start looking at new cars!"

"That's nice," I said. "We're going fishing again. Just about every time it's his turn to plan Family Day, Dad chooses fishing!"

"Sorry," Sara said.

"Why did you say that?"

"I don't really know," she told me. "I guess you didn't sound very enthused!"

"Well, I am enthused!" I told her. "Actually, once you learn to sit still, fishing is lots of fun! Sara, want to work on our quilts tomorrow?"

"Maybe in the afternoon," Sara said. "But Mom and I have plans in the morning. Did I tell you she's cutting back her time at the restaurant?"

For the next several afternoons, Sara and I sat on my porch and sewed. And every day, she'd tell me about Ernie's phone call from the night before. Actually, finding a house in New Jersey wasn't easy! Sara said her mom couldn't believe how much everything costs!

But on Friday, Ernie was back! And he brought with him a picture of Sara's new home. Although it probably isn't as big as Home Sweet Home, it's much nicer. And compared to where Sara lives now, it's huge!

"See the trees?" Sara said. "Ernie says there are lots of tall trees in New Jersey."

"You said there were beaches!"

"That's in another part," Sara explained.

"But doesn't this house cost a lot of money?"

"I guess so! But Ernie worked something out." Sara grinned. "Guess what? It has four bedrooms! And two and a half bathrooms!"

"How could it have half a bathroom?"

"Beats me! When I get there, I'll write and let you know!" Sara grinned. "Guess what?"

"What?"

"We're going to live close to a college!"

"So? That's a long time off, Sara!"

"For me anyway!" A smile covered Sara's face. "Mom's dream is coming true! When I begin school in the fall, Mom's going to start college!"

"No kidding!" I said. "That's wonderful!"

"And, Katie, I've saved the best until last!"

"Don't tell me there's more?"

Sara twirled around with this silly grin on her face. "I really can hardly believe it myself, Katie!" she said. "Just listen to this! We'll be less than an hour away from New York City! Broadway, here I come!"

Sara Gets a Father

All at once, things were happening faster and faster. Every day Sara had something else to be excited about. Not just the dream of Broadway! Now it was her mother's wedding dress. And shopping for her bridesmaid dress. And then something that even got to my brother Jason—a shiny new imported car!

I really tried to show enthusiasm. After all, that's what friends are for! It wasn't that I wasn't happy for Sara. But by comparison, my own life suddenly seemed pretty boring!

Actually, the only thing that didn't work out right away was a place for the wedding. Finally, Mrs. Wilcox came over to ask my mother for suggestions. "We don't need a big place," she said. "I don't have many friends. I met a lot of people at the restaurant. But the only person I really got to know was Ernie!"

"I wish we could have the wedding here," Mom said. "But I'm afraid Home Sweet Home isn't nice enough!" Then she began to smile! "I've got it! Fellowship Hall! I'll take you over there tomorrow. I think it would be perfect!"

"Karen probably has more friends than she thinks she does," Mom said, after Sara's mother went home. "I'd love to give a shower for her! Katie, would you like to help me?"

"Sure," I said. "Can Sara help too?"

"I think Sara's busy enough already," Mom said. "And besides, it isn't polite for people to give showers for their own families! Katie, this will be our special gift for Sara and her mother! Let's do it together."

Well, usually I love things like that. But this time I never really got into it. Oh, I wrote the invitations, and made favors, and helped with the cooking, and set the table. But something was wrong. My heart just wasn't in it.

"The table looks fantastic!" Mom said. "Katie, I love your idea to put the punch in that ironstone bowl!" Carefully we set it at one end of the dining room table, which was covered with a quilt instead of a tablecloth.

The first guests to arrive at the shower were

two other waitresses. Since I had never seen them before, I smiled and tried desperately to think of something to say. But luckily, once Mayblossom arrived, everyone started having fun! Her enthusiasm is catching! "Isn't this exciting!" she said. "Karen will be thrilled! Does Sara suspect anything?"

"I don't think she guessed," I said. "Sara has so much going on now that I don't think she even realized we were getting ready for a party!"

Actually, Sara and her mother were so surprised they nearly fainted! Mrs. Wilcox got plenty of presents, including two toasters. And everyone said it was the best shower they ever went to!

Personally, I had to force myself to smile the whole time. I smiled until my face hurt. But down inside I felt like I wasn't really there!

* * * * * * * *

The wedding itself was small. Very small. Mrs. Wilcox has no family. And Ernie Kennedy has only a brother in Oregon and an aunt and uncle in Missouri he hasn't seen in eleven years. "You'll have to be our family!" they told us.

Fellowship Hall really looked like a garden. I helped Mom arrange baskets of flowers all around the fireplace. And Dad and Jason had set up the chairs to make that end of the room look cozy.

When the music began and Sara came through the door, I gasped! Her long, blue dress was simple, without ruffles or puffed sleeves or anything else that looks babyish. A crown of daisies sat on top of her red curls. She walked slowly—tall and straight. I mean, she could easily have passed for fourteen!

Sara's mother had asked Sam Johnson to walk in with her. In his white coat, he looked so different I hardly knew him! But his white hair and smile were the same. Suddenly, I realized that next time, he would be the groom!

Sara's mother looked young and beautiful! The flowers in her long blond hair matched her pale blue dress. Even without wearing white, she looked just like a bride!

Waiting in front stood the smiling Ernie Kennedy. I had forgotten all about his being so short until the bride and groom turned to face the minister. From the back, they struck me funny, but naturally I wouldn't let myself smile.

The amazing thing was how fast it was over! Suddenly, the minister was introducing Mr. and Mrs. Kennedy! As they stood there smiling, Sara's mother pulled a white rose from her bouquet and handed it to Sara. Then the three of them walked out together!

Outside the church, as Sara walked toward me, suddenly I felt shy. "Sara, you're lovely!" I told her. "You look so mature!"

Sara grinned. "That's exactly what Ernie told me!" Then she corrected herself. "I mean that's what *my father* said! Should I put my suitcase in Purple Jeep?"

While her parents went for a weekend honeymoon in Aspen, Sara stayed with us. Dad had set up a rollaway cot in my room. After we got home from the reception, we went upstairs to put on our pajamas. Sara was very quiet. I realized she had hardly said a word since she joined us.

"It was a super wedding!" I told her. "Your mother looked beautiful and so did you! And I've never seen a happier man than Ernie Kennedy!"

"Can I tell you something?" Now Sara seemed nervous. "Katie, I feel kind of funny! I mean, I couldn't wait to call him Dad. But now when I say it, it sounds really dumb!"

"You just aren't used to the change," I told her. "Actually, I still think of my teacher as Ms. Allen!"

"That's not the only thing that's changing!" Sara said. "Suddenly, as I walked out of the church, it hit me! Katie, my whole life is going to be different!"

"I know."

"I've been so excited. But now it's really sinking in!" she said. "From now on, nothing's going to be the same!"

I grinned. "You have the same mother!"

Sara shook her head. "No, Mom's changing too! I know this is hard to believe, Katie, but this morning my mother left a dirty plate and some silverware in the sink!"

I laughed. "Big deal!"

Sara ignored me. "But at least she's happy. I'm sure of that! And I'm going to try my best to keep it that way!"

"It won't be perfect," I told her. "No family is perfect!"

"Yours is!" Sara said. "I've watched you all year, and I know you're different from any family I've ever seen before!"

"I suppose that's because we're all Christians! But believe me, we certainly aren't perfect!"

"I've already decided something," Sara said. "When I get married, I want to have a Christian home like yours. And who knows? Maybe Mom and Ernie will get interested in God."

"Why not? At least now they have someone to introduce them!"

"I don't know," Sara said. "It's hard to talk about God to your own mother! Not to mention a brand-new father!"

"Sara, let's both keep praying for them! Maybe they'll bring it up! Maybe they'll even ask you about Jesus!"

Sara smiled. "Katie, when that happens, I'll call right away and tell you all about it!"

I smiled too. Frankly, at that very moment I felt better than I had in weeks.

But gradually Sara's smile faded. She shook her head. "It won't be the same for us either," she admitted. "I'm going to miss you, Katie Hooper!"

Before we went to sleep, Sara and I promised each other we'd write letters twice a week. And then we cried our eyes out!

On Monday morning, Sara and I sat on my steps and waited for the newlyweds to return. Their shiny gray car drove up just before lunch.

While I stood there watching, the new Mrs. Kennedy smiled and gave Sara a great big hug.

"Hey," Ernie said, "don't forget she's my daughter too!" Then he hugged her until I thought her stuffing would come out! "Sara, it's so good to be back!" he said. "We've really missed you!"

A smile covered Sara's entire face. "I'm glad you're home!" she said. "I missed you too, *Dad!*"

*Our Script
Is Changed*

Now, as I stood by watching helplessly, the days passed faster and faster. One afternoon a man came to pack everything at Sara's house in boxes. He moved so fast, it was hard just keeping out of his way! So Sara and I hung out in the yard.

"Remember when we sold candy?" I asked. "Sara, how come you're so good at selling things?"

"Beats me!" she said. "Maybe it's a gift!"

"A gift?"

"Sure! Mayblossom says the Lord gives people different gifts!" She grinned. "I think it just means you're better at some things, and I'm better at others!"

"Oh, no!" I said. "Sara, I just realized something! I missed your birthday, didn't I?"

"It's OK, Katie!" She smiled. "This year I had a family celebration!"

"But I was going to give you a party!" I told her. "It was going to be a surprise!"

"You and your mother gave the shower!" she said. "And boy, were we surprised!"

"Sara!" Ernie called. "Can you come here?"

"Coming, Dad!" She turned to me. "Don't leave, Katie! I'll be right back!"

When Sara returned, her mother was with her. "Hi, Katie!" said Mrs. Kennedy. "Is your mom home?"

"I think so," I said.

"The packer's almost finished," Mrs. Kennedy said. "We want to say good-bye. It will be harder to get away tomorrow!"

While Sara and I watched, our mothers stood in my kitchen and hugged each other. "Elizabeth, I can never thank you enough!" Sara's mother said.

"Thank me? What for?" Mom asked.

"For all you've done for Sara!" her mother said. "While I was working such long hours, you gave her a home base! You've taught her to cook. And to sew. I think she's learned a lot about babies! And she's always really enjoyed going to church with you!"

Sara and I looked at each other and smiled.

"And there's something else," Mrs. Kennedy said. "I think the Hoopers have showed us what being a family is all about!"

Mom smiled. "We love Sara! Having her here has been fun for all of us! But it's been wonderful for Katie! She never had a real friend before!"

"I didn't either!" Sara said.

"Remember in the beginning?" I asked. "When we just moved in? Remember how excited we were when we found the treasure!"

"And I almost missed out, because I was so afraid of the ghost!" Sara giggled.

"We never did get our skis!" I realized.

"But we sure had fun earning money for them!" Sara looked at her mother. "I wonder if there's skiing in New Jersey?"

"Don't ask me!" Mrs. Kennedy laughed. "I've never been there either!"

"Karen, how your life has changed!" Mom said.

"I know. Sometimes I can hardly believe it myself!" Mrs. Kennedy shook her head. "I really thought when my first husband died that my dreams died too!"

"We're so happy for you!" Mom told her. "But we're going to miss you a lot!"

"We'll miss you too!" Karen smiled. "But don't

121

worry! We'll see each other again! I mean, if you're ever in New Jersey ..."

"Right!" Mom said softly. I watched her face. And I knew right then and there that she thought it never was going to happen!

"If you have a chance, stop by tomorrow," Karen told us.

"I'll be there, Sara," I promised. She nodded. Now neither of us was smiling.

"We'd better go, Sara," her mother said. "Your dad's waiting to take us out for a hamburger!"

By the time I got to Sara's the next morning, a huge moving van filled the road. Frankly, it looked bigger than Sara's house! Two men were building a ramp up to a door in the side.

"I'm so excited I could hardly eat!" Sara said. She was nearly dancing up and down. "But Dad told me I'd need my strength for the trip!"

I was surprised. "You're leaving today? I thought you were staying to clean the house!"

Sara grinned. "Dad says there's nothing to clean! If things go well, he's hoping to drive 300 miles before tonight!"

"So, I guess you'll be sleeping in a motel," I said. "I've never slept in a motel!"

"Me either! Katie, I'll write a letter and tell you all about it!"

"When will you get there?" I asked. "To New Jersey, I mean?"

"I'm not sure. But Dad starts his job on Monday. Mom says I'll have to help her when the movers deliver our stuff!"

Together we sat down on the curb. Suddenly, I started to giggle. "Remember our diets?"

"I'll never eat lemon Jell-O again!" Sara laughed.

"Or lime!" I said. "Lime was worse!"

We watched the men carry out the huge television set. When I first met Sara, she used to watch it all the time. "I wonder if you'll have the same television programs in New Jersey?"

"Probably," Sara said. "But our news will be different. And Dad says everything's two hours later than here!"

"How come?"

"Beats me! I'll write and tell you when I find out!"

Now we just sat and watched. A man struggled with a huge mattress box.

"Katie, you'll have to write and let me know what happens to Calvin Young!" Sara said.

"I thought you said you didn't like him!"

"Oh, Calvin's all right." She grinned. "As it turns out, I'm probably a lot better off without any long-term relationships!"

"Hey, maybe we can both go to the same college!" I said suddenly.

"Right. Maybe we can!"

"Unless by then you're on Broadway!"

"It won't matter!" Sara told me. "No matter what, I'm still going to college! Don't forget you promised me you'll go too!"

"I promise," I said.

Her eyes got big. "College is very important, Katie!"

I nodded. For a few minutes we just sat there. Then I giggled. "Sara, every time I see a Christmas pageant, I'll think of you!"

She laughed too. "When reporters ask me about my very first role on the stage, I'll tell them I was the Chief Angel!"

I blinked back tears. "Sara, don't go!"

"I have no choice!" she said.

Suddenly, the small house was empty. And the men were closing up the truck. And Mrs. Kennedy was carrying the vacuum out to the car. After that, Sara's mother hugged me. Then so did Sara's father. And at last I was left standing alone on the sidewalk with my best friend.

When it came right down to saying good-bye, Sara Wilcox and I just stood and looked at each other.

"I'll miss you, Sara," I told her.

"Me too! Promise you'll write?"

I promised. So did she.

"Come on, Sara!" her mother called.

"I love you, Katie Hooper!" she said. Tears

125

were running down her cheeks.

"Me too!" I said, with tears running down my own cheeks.

We hugged. And then Sara Wilcox ran over and climbed into the shiny gray car. Both of us waved until it turned out of sight.

I just stood there all alone and cried my eyes out.

Lord, this wasn't how it was supposed to end! Why, next year Sara and I were going to learn to ski! And we were going out for cheerleading! Naturally, we'd both get boyfriends. And in high school we were going to double date! And we were going to study hard so we'd both get college scholarships! She was supposed to be the maid of honor at my wedding! Of course, I planned to name my first girl Sara! And naturally, she'd name hers Katie!

With tears still running down my face, I turned and started walking toward my house. Well, maybe I could still do it! Name my first girl Sara, I mean!

I Stop
Crying – Finally!

Actually, I spent the next two days crying. I mean, I used up entire boxes of Kleenex! Just when I'd think I was OK, tears would fill my eyes again. Even praying didn't seem to help. "It just isn't worth it, Lord!" I told Him. "I'm never going to get close to anybody again!"

Finally, Mom suggested that maybe I'd feel better if I'd do something! But the trouble was, everything I tried reminded me of Sara Wilcox!

When I babysat at Stones', I remembered how Sara made the toddlers march around the church nursery. I tried taking pictures, but all I could think of was doing it together at the wedding. Actually, Sara had filled every part of my life!

Except jogging! Now that was an idea! I put on my shoes, called January, and headed off. And the first time I did it, I saw Christopher Bean!

"Katie, I didn't think you were running anymore," he said.

"I haven't run for a long time," I admitted. "Did you have a good time on your trip?"

"I did. But it's good to be back!" he said. "I hear Sara Wilcox is moving!"

"She's already gone!" My eyes filled with tears. It was embarrassing.

"I'm sorry, Katie!" Christopher said. "To be honest, I'm usually the one who moves! I never realized it was so hard to be left behind!"

"It's awful!" I told him. "It's like ... like somebody turned off the lights!" Where had I heard that?

"Are you tired?" He slowed down too.

"Kind of." I looked down. "To be honest, I don't really feel like running anymore."

"I understand," he said. "I'm out every morning. I'll stop for you if you want me to."

"Thanks," I told him.

On Sunday, the kids in Sara's Sunday-school class wondered how she's doing. At Mayblossom's suggestion, they had prayed for her.

"She's probably just getting to New Jersey," I said. "Naturally, she couldn't write while she was traveling!"

By then I had already written three letters. I hoped the post office would save them for her. After all, Sara would miss me too! I just hoped she wouldn't think my letters were dumb! After all, not much is happening in Woodland Park.

Early Monday morning the phone rang, and Mom handed me the telephone. It was Kimberly Harris. "Hi, Katie!" she said. "I've been trying to reach you for a couple of weeks!"

"I know," I admitted. "I've been involved. Did you know Sara Wilcox just moved away?"

"That's what I heard," she said. "Some of the girls were talking about it."

"Some of what girls?" I asked.

"Some of the girls from our class at school. I might as well tell you," she said. "Last week I had a slumber party. I was really hoping you could come, Katie, but I understand. Mom said you've been awfully busy!"

I just stood there for a second. "Kimberly, I'm sorry I didn't call you back! I don't even have a good excuse! Will you forgive me?"

She laughed. "Of course, silly! I didn't take it personally! I always knew Sara was your best friend."

"I'm beginning to see that having a best friend isn't always the greatest!" I said. "I mean, if she goes, it's terrible!"

"When I moved here, I left a best friend in

Philadelphia," Kimberly told me. "That's one of the reasons I was so excited to go back."

"So," I said, "was it cool getting together again?"

"Real cool!" she said. She paused. "Oh, Katie, with you I think I can be honest!"

"It wasn't cool?"

"It was horrible!" she said. "Even worse than horrible!"

"So, what happened?"

"Lisa's so self-centered!" Kimberly said. "All she ever talked about is what's happening in Philadelphia. And her new boyfriend!"

"She's changed?"

"A lot! Well, I guess I've changed too! Actually, Katie, this may surprise you, but you've had a big influence on my life!"

"I have?"

"Actually, for most of the year, you were the only friend I had! I watched you. You're different, Katie. You always see the good in people. And you're so cheerful!"

"I am?" I forced a laugh. "I haven't been too cheerful lately!"

"So? Nobody's perfect!"

"Only Jesus," I said, softly.

"What did you say?"

"Nothing." Suddenly, I remembered the first time I told Sara about Jesus. I wonder if Kimberly might like to visit our Sunday school?

"Katie, could I come over this afternoon?" she asked. "I've been wanting to tell you what happened when I went over to your cousin's!"

"Kimberly's coming over!" I told Mom.

Mom smiled. "Another best friend?"

"I don't think so," I said slowly. "From now on, I'm going to try to have lots of friends!"

What surprised me was how much Kimberly Harris has changed! Was this something new? I wondered why I hadn't noticed it before. Maybe at the time I was just too involved with Sara Wilcox. Of course, Kimberly's nothing like Sara! So what?

That afternoon, Kimberly Harris and I sat on my back porch, and I worked on my quilt. "I was so disappointed when you told me you didn't talk to Jennifer," I said. "It wasn't too realistic, but I had this dream that my cousin and I would get together!"

"They were out of town," Kimberly said.

"Oh? How did you find that out?"

"I kept phoning, but no one answered. So one day Lisa's mother drove me over there." She smiled. "You see, Lisa had a date!"

"No kidding!"

"Well, anyhow, your cousin lives in a beautiful house," Kimberly said. "It's huge—bigger than mine! And it's set in the woods."

"No kidding!" I said. "It's too bad nobody was home!"

Kimberly grinned. "No, but listen to this! While I was walking around, this *hunk* came over from across the street!" Now she grinned from ear to ear.

"A boy?"

"More like a man! Anyhow, he told me he's Matthew Harrington! I guess the Harringtons are good friends of the Greens! They go to the same church or something." Kimberly couldn't stop smiling.

"Do you think he's Jennifer's boyfriend?"

"If he is, she's a lucky girl!" Kimberly grinned. "Well, anyhow, when I said I was a friend of Jennifer's cousin, he said he'd tell her I stopped by! I hope it was OK. I even gave him your address!"

"So I still might hear from her?" Now I was smiling. It felt good to be smiling again!

"Katie, I love your quilt!" Kimberly said. "I've always wanted to make a quilt!"

Suddenly, I remembered Sara. And I found myself wondering if she would ever finish the quilt she started. I smiled at Kimberly. "I could show you how!"

"Would you?" she asked. "But first, I'm making myself a dress for the first day of school!"

I was surprised. "You can make a dress?"

"A simple one," Kimberly said. "Actually, working with patterns isn't very difficult. Katie, if you want to make something yourself, I'm sure my mother would show you how!"

I laughed. "I don't know. Mom's tried, but she hasn't had any success teaching me! She's given up more than once!"

Kimberly nodded. "That's because she's your own mother!" she said. "Sometimes it's easier to learn from somebody else's!"

"You really think I could do it?"

"Of course!" She smiled at me. "Katie, anybody who can sew a quilt by hand can certainly learn to make a dress!"

"I'll do it!" I said. I took a deep breath. And then I could feel a smile spreading across my face. Somehow I knew I could finally stop carrying around that stupid box of Kleenex. Because now I had something to look forward to!

My Life Goes Into Orbit!

Boring? Nothing happening? Don't make me laugh! Before the next weekend rolled around, my life was spinning so fast I could hardly keep my balance!

The same night after Kimberly came over, Dad was so excited he could hardly wait until my brother finished reading Romans 12. "Kids, we have some news," he said.

"Not another baby!" I blurted out.

Dad didn't wait for any more guesses. "Are you guys ready for another adventure?" He grinned. "The bank has sold this property, and Home Sweet Home is going to be torn down!"

"Oh, no!" Jason said. "Here we go again!"

Mom smiled. "It isn't going to be like last

time!" she assured us. "We already have a new home! You know that huge Victorian on the way to the high school? The blue one?"

"We can afford that?" my brother asked.

"We won't be buying it," Dad said. "Mr. Stone has a client who will pay us to live there. They want us to turn it into a Bed and Breakfast!"

"What's that?" I asked.

"It's like a hotel," Mom explained. "Tourists will pay to sleep in the extra bedrooms and stay for breakfast." She couldn't stop smiling. "Of course, we can do it only if you kids are willing to help!"

"It sounds like fun!" I said. "But I sure hope it has more than one bathroom!" Actually, it does! And it looks like we'll be moving in before winter!

I couldn't wait to tell Kimberly! She and her mother picked me up the next afternoon. And by the time I got home, I had material, pattern, thread, zipper, and buttons for a new blue dress!

"Can you come tomorrow to cut it out?" Mrs. Harris asked. "Katie, how about if I pick you up? Can you join us for lunch?"

Well, by noon the next day, Kimberly had more news! "Pam O'Grady called last night," she told me. "She and Michelle are starting a club. They want us to be in it!"

"They want me too?" I couldn't believe it.

"Pam tried to call you, but she said the line was always busy!"

I laughed. "We are getting lots of calls! Unfortunately, most of them are for Jason!"

"Not for long!" Kimberly said, grinning. "Guess what? I hear Calvin Young likes you!"

"I know," I said. "As a matter of fact, he's been teasing me ever since kindergarten."

"I don't mean that Calvin just likes you." She grinned again. "I mean he *likes* you!"

I grinned too. It wasn't cool, but I couldn't help it. "How do you know?" I asked.

"He told Christopher Bean, and Christopher told me! We've been pals since the field trip. Actually, Christopher was asking my advice. He likes you too, Katie! He says you're sensitive!"

"Christopher told you he likes me? Are you kidding!" Now I couldn't stop smiling.

That evening, I did get a telephone call, but it wasn't from Calvin or Christopher. It was Mayblossom McDuff. "Hi, Katie! How are you doing?"

"Pretty good now," I said.

"Have you heard from Sara?"

"Not yet. And I wrote her three letters."

"Give her time," she said. "She's probably still snowed under! I found out that moving's a lot of work!" Mayblossom laughed her tinkling little laugh. "Katie, I called to ask you something.

Sam and I don't see any reason to wait a long time before we get married. We're trying to get the church early in October. And I was wondering if you'd be a bridesmaid?"

"Me?" I couldn't believe it. "You mean with a special dress and everything?"

"Of course! How about it, Katie?"

"Sure!" I said. "If it's OK with Mom."

"How about if I ask her?"

I was dancing up and down. Kind of like Sara used to do. "Mom!" I called. I hung around listening until Mom started talking about the Bed and Breakfast. Then I went up to my room. I looked at the stenciled hearts around the ceiling. And the birthday drawings of me Dad sketches every year. In a few weeks, this room would be history! Along with everything else that happened in this house during the past year.

"Katie!" Mom called. "Telephone!"

I raced down. Maybe it was Sara Wilcox!

"Katie?" said a voice I didn't recognize.

"Yes. This is Katie Hooper!"

"Oh, great!" she said. "This is your cousin, Jennifer Green!"

"Where are you?" I asked.

She laughed. "Where else? In Pennsylvania!"

"You sound so close!"

"Matthew Harrington told me your friend

stopped by while we were away on vacation!"

"Her name is Kimberly Harris," I said.

"Whatever! Anyhow, I decided to call!" She sure sounded nice! "Katie, no offense, but all my life I've been curious about you! I've always wondered what Aunt Elizabeth's children would be like!"

I felt embarrassed. "I've wondered about you too. Mom says you have two younger brothers."

"Pete and Justin," she told me. "How about you? I think you have a brother too."

"Mine's older. His name is Jason. Did you know we have a baby named Amy?"

"No kidding! A baby! I can't believe it!"

"She's almost a year old," I said.

"And you live in a mountain cabin, right?"

"Not anymore," I said. "Now we live in an old wreck of a place. But it's getting torn down. Next we're moving to a Bed and Breakfast!"

"Perfect!" she said. "Will you have room for us to stay with you?"

"You're coming here?" I asked. "When?"

"Dad's always promising," Jennifer said. "But if I really bug him, I know we'll get there!"

"Please, don't come yet!" I said. "Please wait until we move!"

Jennifer laughed. "Don't worry! We'll let you know!" There was a pause. "Katie, is there anything you'd like to ask me?"

"Kind of," I said. I blurted it out. "Do you really have a boyfriend?"

She laughed. "I have several! Why?"

"I just wondered." I took a deep breath. "Jennifer, please tell me about my grandmother!"

Jennifer's voice got soft. "Grandma Green's the greatest grandmother in the whole world!" she said. "Katie, she'd love to get to know you!"

"Mom says my father is stubborn," I said. "But, Jennifer, please don't tell anybody!"

"I think they already know," she said. "Hey, I have to go now. Can I call you again?"

"Sure! I'd like that a lot!"

I couldn't wait to tell Mom. But my news didn't make her happy. To be honest, she cried!

Although my life was getting more and more busy, I still kept watching the mailbox for a letter from Sara. She promised she'd write! I couldn't believe she'd forgotten already!

And then the next day, when I wasn't even looking, I got two letters! One had a star next to the return address. It was Sara's symbol!

Dear Katie!

Please forgive me for not writing sooner! I never dreamed moving was such a big deal! Our house is so big we rattle around in it! By the way, Mom is still very neat! You're right. Some things never change! Dad likes his job

a lot! He has a very nice boss named Larry!
My neighborhood is full of girls about my
age! Their names are: Nikole, Robin, Mela-
nie, and Rachel. They invited me to join
their club. How come we never thought of
having a club? People do ski in New Jersey,
but you'd laugh at what they call moun-
tains! Guess what? We're getting tickets to
Phantom of the Opera! (BROADWAY!) I
miss you a lot! Please write!

Your friend, Sara

I smiled. She didn't mention my letters, but
she must have received them. Actually, now I
have tons more stuff to tell her. I just hope I can
find time to write her back!

The second letter was written in small, neat
handwriting. There was no return address. I
stuck my finger in and torn open the envelope.

My dear granddaughter, Katie!

If you could only know how often I've
wanted to contact you! Now Jennifer tells me
she actually talked to you! And I just can't
wait any longer! Life is too short!

Katie, please show this letter to your par-
ents! Tell them I love them both. And I ask
your father to forgive me for opposing their
marriage. Obviously, we were wrong! God is
in control, and He is blessing you!

140

Can't we make a new start! Please may I come for a visit?

With Jesus' love,
Grandma Green

Although I could hardly stand it, I waited until bedtime to show the letter to my parents. As I watched Mom's face, I was pretty sure what would happen. Sure enough, tears filled her eyes. Without a word, she handed the letter to my father.

But what happened next was a total surprise. Dad, my always smiling father, actually burst into tears! I could hardly handle it. But when I started to leave the room, Mom shook her head.

Finally, Dad spoke. "Elizabeth, I loved you so much!" he said. "I can't tell you how it hurt when your parents didn't accept me! But it was wrong for me to make you choose between us! God never gives choices like that! Darling, will you forgive me?"

Well, of course, Mom did forgive him. And I did too! And now the greatest thing in the world is going to happen! My real grandmother, my very own Grandma Green, is coming to visit us in Colorado!

* * * * * * * *

Well, pardon me, but actually, I'm kind of in a

rush! As you can see, my life in Woodland Park is far from boring! But I do know this: No matter what happens from now on, I'll never forget that year with Sara Wilcox! I don't think I ever could. I just hope when Sara thinks back over her life, she'll remember she once had a best friend named Katie Hooper!